RANCH FEUD

Doc Beck Westerns Book 5

SARAH ELISABETH SAWYER

Only the moon lit the giant pines hovering above Trey Wallace as he sat horseback in the foothills of the Medicine Bow Mountains. The light from the main house at the McKinnon Ranch sure couldn't reach him. The house sat far below, two miles away from where he hid among the loblolly branches.

No one in that uppity crowd descending from buggies and wagons or on horseback would ever know he watched them.

Trey leaned forward and crossed his arms on the saddle horn, letting his fingers dangle loose with the reins. He spoke to his horse Dixie, the only one who cared about listening to him.

"Well, little lady, that's a big to-do they're having. Not surprised they didn't invite the Wallace clan. Wouldn't have been room for us anyway, not with those Butlers there."

His mare twitched her ears back to catch the sound of his voice then pricked forward again, alert to the sounds of the night.

But Trey didn't take his eyes off the two-story mansion that stood on its own little hill. Valleys lay between Trey on his high spot and the mansion, the last dip littered with a barn, corrals, and bunkhouse. Doc McKinnon had a fine spread, a real cattle king in this Wyoming territory.

Correction—Wyoming *state*, something Trey still wasn't used to after growing up in Wyoming *territory*. There was a difference, his pa said.

But statehood or not, there would never be true civilization in this wild country as long as the likes of Glenn Butler was courted and favored. Something else his pa said.

Trey and his father wouldn't be welcome at that shindig, for sure. Folks in Centennial Ridge and the surrounding ranches looked on the Wallace clan like cur dogs. Even Doc McKinnon, who Trey's father had once called an honest man, sided with the Butlers in public. What rankled Trey most was how Doctor Rebekah LaRoche took to the Butlers last year.

Trey clenched the reins, causing his mare to flinch. He eased off and smiled to himself. Doctor Rebekah LaRoche thought she was smart in sending off a recommendation letter for Lilly Butler, Glenn Butler's daughter, getting the girl in some fancy school back east. They all thought they were smug and progressive. Trey didn't care no more about that than the party taking place at the house he stared at for an hour now.

His mare pricked her ears again. Maybe she heard his long sigh. But when her head came up, Trey knew it was more than that.

Dixie looked south, inhaling and then exhaling with a soft whinny. Trey gave her a pat on the neck and loosened the reins. He nudged her forward, letting her follow her instincts.

She picked up a trot and found a game trail down the hillside. Only this wasn't a game trail. It was too wide.

In the moonlight that barely showed the way, Trey reckoned it was a trail used by the McKinnon horse herds that free-roamed in the mountains. Doc McKinnon was not only a cattle king—he maintained one of the largest horse herds in the county. In the whole blamed state.

When the trail leveled in a gully and they broke through a thicket of quaking aspens, Trey pulled his mare to a halt. A sound reached his human ears. A sound he didn't like at all.

Thunder reverberated from the clear night sky, echoing through the foothills.

Before Trey could spin Dixie around, a herd of horses surged over the rise to his right, their hooves churning earth and beating down the summer prairie grasses.

Charging alongside them was a man on horseback, waving his yellow rain slicker in an attempt to turn the herd uphill and slow them. The moon flashed on his silver hatband and Trey recognized it along with the perpetual slouch of the fellow's shoulders.

It was Ol' Mosby, head wrangler on the McKinnon Ranch. He was the man who had gifted Dixie to Trey when Mosby worked for the Wallace outfit.

Ol' Mosby succeeded in partially turning the herd toward the hills, but if they angled toward the open gully in front of Trey, there'd be no stopping them from charging into the dark mountains.

Trey whipped up Dixie to get in the gap and help turn the horse herd. He whipped off his brown Stetson and waved it wildly at the herd while yipping like a coyote.

The lead horse shied away from him, slowing the galloping charge. There were at least 100 horses in the stampede and they looked to be calming after their run over the hill. As they passed Trey at a lope, he looked up to see Ol' Mosby sitting with the rain slicker slack at his side.

Mosby dropped the slicker and yanked his rifle out of the scabbard. Whether or not the aging cowboy recognized Trey Wallace wouldn't matter. If Mosby thought there was a lone man up to no good on the McKinnon ranch, he'd shoot. If he knew it was Trey Wallace snooping around, he'd likely shoot, too. He hadn't left the Wallace outfit on good terms.

Trey pulled his hat back on his head and started to reach for his gun when a shot ripped through the air.

Mosby's slouched shoulder jerked and he dropped his rifle to clutch his saddle horn in an attempt to stay upright. His horse took off at a gallop as the herd picked up their run again, galloping toward the foothills.

Four riders came over the rise, weapons drawn and wearing bandanas over their faces. They spotted Trey.

Trey drew his gun as a bullet sang by his ear. It wasn't a tune he wanted to hear again, but Ol' Mosby would be dead for sure if Trey turned tail and ran.

The Wallaces never ran.

Trey fired off two quick rounds at the riders who were coming down the hill at him.

Ol' Mosby's trotting horse was almost even with Trey now and he pushed Dixie forward enough to grab the reins of the man's horse.

Kicking Dixie in the sides, he charged up the hill separating the gully from the McKinnon valley. Trey glanced back for two reasons: to see if the men were pursuing them and if Ol' Mosby was still in the saddle.

The answer to the first was no, the second yes.

The horse rustlers were going after the herd. Trey couldn't stop them, but he could get Mosby out of there. And maybe Doc McKinnon would wish he'd sent an invitation to the Wallace clan after all.

Contrary to the gossip in that territory, this Wallace was from good stock.

CHAPTER 1

"I'm awful sorry, Miss Rebekah."

Jimmy kept a gentle grip on Rebekah's elbow as he helped her to the wall. She limped along beside him, weaving between dancers enjoying the rest of the tune.

Oh my darling, oh my darling
Oh my darling, Clementine
You are lost and gone forever
Dreadful sorry, Clementine

Rebekah attempted to pry Jimmy's fingers loose when they reached the wall as she turned to face the party inside Doctor Robert McKinnon's home.

"It's all right, Jimmy. You're learning."

Her sore toe would be fine. So would Jimmy's embarrassment of accidentally stepping on her foot while she was trying to teach him to dance at this—his first birthday party.

The dance ended and everyone gave a ruckus applause for the small orchestra set up in one corner of the parlor. Most of the furnishings were removed that morning by gleeful ranch hands in anticipation of the big celebration.

Though Jimmy had only been at the McKinnon Ranch a few weeks, he made fast friends. Besides, people in rural Wyoming were more than happy for any reason to have a party in this dry start to the summer.

The crystal chandelier hanging from the twelve-foot ceiling gave the room a festive glow to match everyone's best, whether they were upper crust or tenant farmers. Doctor McKinnon excluded no one from his gatherings based on social status. It was one of many things Rebekah admired about her uncle.

Jimmy still had a hold of her elbow, but he was facing the gathering too, his eyes glowing like they had all day. He said from the side of his mouth, "This ranch is just about the finest place this side of heaven, Miss Rebekah."

Rebekah smiled and finally succeeded in loosening his fingers from her elbow. It hurt worse than her throbbing toe.

He looked at her, grinning. "Doc McKinnon is an awful smart man. He can answer any question in the world and I've asked most of them since I saw his library. And he's kind, too. Is he really your uncle? I ain't heard you call him it except once, when we first got here."

Rebekah knew the shadow crossing her face was visible to Jimmy because he winced. But she wouldn't let any dark shadows spoil his special night.

"It's a long story, Jimmy. I'll tell you about it someday."

She didn't add that her sudden shadow was from the memory of what she returned to the ranch from—being held captive by Sancho Guerra and his horrible family—not her complex history.

The orchestra struck up another tune and Rebekah nudged Jimmy. "Why don't you ask one of the young ladies to dance? There are several here and I know they would enjoy meeting you."

She hadn't meant to cause Jimmy to blush so deeply. He looked at the far corner where a gaggle of silly teenage girls were whispering behind their hands and batting eyelashes his way.

Whether he was in his dusty mustard yellow jacket or dressed up as he was tonight with a starched white shirt, tan trousers, suspenders, and string tie, Jimmy was a fine-looking young man.

Jimmy looked away quickly from the corner and down at his polished tan boots, rocking back on his heels, sinking them deep in the plush burgundy carpet. "Aw, come on, Miss Rebekah. I'd just step on their toes and they likely wouldn't be as forgiving as you."

His words struck Rebekah oddly, but she didn't know why.

Forgiving.

That was it. Was she really a forgiving person?

This wasn't the time to ponder it. Two people were making their way toward Rebekah around the crowd. She hadn't seen the Butlers yet and guessed they arrived late, which was strange for the normally prompt family.

Glenn Butler and his daughter Lilly out dressed everyone at the party. Rebekah guessed the young woman's dress was purchased in Washington, D.C. where she was attending college. It certainly hadn't come from the milliner shop in the frontier city of Centennial Ridge, Wyoming.

But the leg of mutton satin sleeves on Lilly's plum colored dress and rosette lace on her bodice didn't brighten her pained expression. She looked worried, which was highly unusual for the confident young woman.

Glenn Butler wore his smile that put even his friends at ill-ease. It seemed even tighter than usual. Lilly clung to his arm, almost as though she would fall over if he weren't holding her tight next to him.

Glenn Butler greeted them with, "Well, Miss Rebekah, it certainly is good to have you back in the territory. What a fine welcome home party."

Rebekah nodded a greeting to Lilly, then said, "Thank you,

Mr. Butler, many people have so graciously welcomed me home..." *How sweet that word: home!* "...but this is actually a birthday party for my friend, Jimmy. Jimmy, this is Mr. Glenn Butler and his daughter, Lilly."

At this, Lilly finally lifted her eyes to meet Rebekah's. Jimmy blushed all the way to his shirt collar as he exchanged greetings with them.

Rebekah said to Lilly, "It's good to see you, dear. How was your last semester before summer break? I imagine you're eager to return this fall. You will graduate in the spring, correct?"

Lilly's eyes darted from Rebekah and up to her father. He didn't return his daughter's look while she seemed to plead for help. Glenn Butler's smile tightened yet more, and then he forced relaxation in his lips.

"Indeed, she is," he said. "Of course, we hope you can attend, Rebekah. If not for your outstanding letter of recommendation, Lilly wouldn't have been accepted at the college, even after her high marks in prep school. They only take a select few students each year and she had been declined twice. We'll be forever indebted to you."

Rebekah cocked her head, wondering at Glenn Butler's long explanation of things she already knew. More so, she was concerned about Lilly's lack of response. The last time Rebekah had seen her was during Christmas break when the young woman talked nonstop for hours about the things she was learning and how much she enjoyed it, and how she truly appreciated Rebekah's help.

But there was a ghostly look in Lilly's eyes tonight. She refused to look at Rebekah. She let the silence linger, giving Lilly an opportunity to speak up. She didn't.

Rebekah finally said, "It was my pleasure to write the letter. Lilly is an exemplary young woman. I know she'll make a fine lawyer, and I can only hope she returns to Wyoming to practice if the lure of the east isn't too much."

The tightness returned to Glenn Butler's smile and he seemed at a loss for words.

While Rebekah debated whether to break the awkward silence or simply excuse herself to visit the punch bowl, Doctor McKinnon came to Glenn Butler's other side.

Butler instantly regained his composure. Doctor McKinnon greeted him warmly, shaking his hand. "Well, you old horse thief, I see you and your lovely daughter—who compensates for all your faults—have decided to join us at last."

Butler returned the handshake firmly. "I thought you might be cross at me for outfoxing you on that horse contract. But the cavalry does deserve the best stock."

Doctor McKinnon chuckled and released Butler's hand. "If I didn't lose to you once a year in business, beating you the rest of the time wouldn't hold the same satisfaction."

The rivals shared a congenial laugh, and then darkness came over Butler's face. "You can beat me any day of the week, Robert, as long as one of us is keeping Dean Wallace's head under water, along with his scurvy lot."

Rebekah knew her own expression turned frosty at the rude comment. Doctor McKinnon hid his disapproval more but he did sober.

"I know you and Dean have been at it since the war," Doctor McKinnon said. "But 30 years is a long time to hold a grudge, Glenn. Maybe it's time to extend an olive branch. We are a civilized state now, not a wild territory filled with rustlers and vigilante justice."

Glenn Butler crossed arms, forcing Lilly to drop her hand. Rebekah couldn't help watching her, even though she knew it made the young woman uncomfortable. Something else was wrong.

Glenn Butler's voice went up a notch. "You can tell that to Dean Wallace, but you might as well be talking to your boot. He's made threats about that contract, claiming I undercut him just for spite. Well, he's right. But if he extends an olive branch with an apology for stealing my ranch when I was near dead after the war, I'll think about accepting it."

Rebekah hated the tension that popped in their small circle as Jimmy stood there, sinking his boot heels in the carpet again, eyes down. He didn't know anything about the history that birthed hatred between Dean Wallace and Glenn Butler, nothing about the decades of bad blood between the families.

But none of that mattered there at Jimmy's birthday party. Suddenly, Rebekah's toe wasn't bothering her one bit and she took Jimmy's arm, startling him.

"If you all will excuse us, I've saved this next dance for Jimmy."

He looked at her in surprise, but grinned. "Whatever you say, Miss Rebekah."

They stayed to the edge of the dancers and Rebekah kept Jimmy angled to where she could watch the Butlers. She saw one of the McKinnon Ranch's top hands, Steve Bowers, approach to ask the beautiful young lady for a dance. Apparently, she declined because he shuffled away alone. Lilly seemed glued to her father's side while he engaged Doctor McKinnon in what Rebekah assumed was more business and political talk.

The dance was a slow one and Rebekah managed to keep her toes free of injury through to the last note. Jimmy let out a gust of air and Rebekah patted him on the shoulder.

"You could have asked Lilly Butler to dance."

A blush came over Jimmy's face again. "She's awful sophisticated and pretty. But not as much as you, Miss Rebekah, of course."

Rebekah gave Jimmy a light hug, knowing what her father used to say was true. One didn't need to be blood kin with someone to feel like they were. She glanced over at Doctor McKinnon.

The family bond was deep enough.

Rebekah was startled when someone tapped Jimmy on the shoulder beside her. She looked up in Laramie Jones's face where he stood with his classic, western man smile. He bowed slightly at the waist.

"Mind if I cut in?" His question was directed at Jimmy.

Jimmy took a big step back with a grin. "Yes, sir. I was just about to go see what Steve is up to."

Jimmy must have left, but Rebekah didn't really notice as the orchestra took up a waltz and Laramie Jones offered her his hand. She took it, smiling up at him as the dance began. Laramie was a good dancer for a former U.S. cavalry officer-turned-cowboy, and she never felt quite as safe as she did with him.

She spoke first as the dance got underway. "I've been so aloof since returning that I haven't properly thanked you for how you've taken Jimmy under your wing the past few weeks. He looks quite debonair in the outfit you bought him."

Laramie grinned. "Don't say that in front of the boys. But Jimmy's one hard worker. He has a natural way with horses, and follows after the Lord like a boy galloping his favorite pony across the wide-open prairie. You did right bringing him back to the ranch."

Rebekah swallowed, feeling a sudden surge of tears in her throat. "It was actually you who brought us both home. I haven't properly thanked you for that, either."

Laramie slowed a beat, putting them out of rhythm with the music, but it didn't matter. "You know I couldn't have left you out there, Becka. As long as I'm breathing, I'll look out for you and I know you'll do the same for me. We always have, haven't we?"

Rebekah nodded, her eyes dropping to the buttons of his starched cream shirt. Laramie Jones—or as she had always known him, Lee Stafford—would give his life for her and she for him.

The sweet moment of the past and present glowing between them was shattered by a crash in the foyer. Not everyone noticed at first, but Laramie Jones was always attuned to any threats. He jerked away from Rebekah to turn and face the wide entrance to the parlor.

Someone blocked Rebekah's view. But then the pathway cleared and she stared at the doorway to see Trey Wallace standing there with Ol' Mosby. The McKinnon ranch wrangler had his limp arm around Trey's shoulders as the younger man held him upright.

They were both dusty and worn-looking. Blood dripped onto the floor.

CHAPTER 2

Trey Wallace glared around the party as though everyone in the room had personally offended him that evening.

His eyes landed on Rebekah and he snarled, "Well, Doc Beck, are you going to treat one of your own or is he too sullied because a Wallace man saved his life?"

Eyes closed, Ol' Mosby's knees gave out and he slumped to the floor.

Laramie and Steve rushed forward to catch him before he hit too hard. Trey relinquished his hold and took a step back.

Rebekah was already in motion, hurrying to the other side of the room and intercepting Jimmy where he had gone forward to help.

He was pale, the joy momentarily gone from his eyes, replaced with worry. Since Jimmy was good with horses, he no doubt had gotten close to Mosby.

Rebekah grabbed his arm. "Jimmy, run up to my room and fetch my medical bag please. It's in the wardrobe."

Jimmy responded instantly. "Be right back, ma'am."

He found a path around the crowd and squeezed through the

doorway past Trey, who gave him a hard look. Jimmy scooted by and bounded up the grand staircase in the foyer.

Rebekah made her way to the sofa pushed against the wall to clear the dance room floor. She'd been right in knowing that was where Laramie would bring the wounded man. She quickly grabbed a blanket off the back of the sofa and spread it over the velvet material to give Mosby a comfortable place to lay.

Laramie supported Mosby on one side with Steve on his other. They lowered the aging cowboy onto the sofa and Rebekah gently lifted his legs as they laid him down. She moved forward to examine the old cowboy. She needed to determine where the blood was coming from.

A quick look told her he was bleeding from his back.

Laramie straightened to look at Trey, saying in his cavalry-captain voice, "What happened?"

Rebekah directed Steve and one of the other ranch hands to carefully turn Mosby over. While they did so, she glanced up to see Trey Wallace leaned on the doorframe. He was limber and light-muscled, one foot crossed over the other, his arms folded as though he were having a casual Saturday conversation with a friend on a street corner. But Rebekah recognized his underlying malice.

"You'll have to ask Ol' Mosby that," Trey said. "All I know is there were four men shooting at him and stampeding the horse herd, and if it hadn't been for me, he'd be dead."

Rebekah carefully held Mosby's head as Steve and the other hand got him positioned on his stomach. Mosby's eyes flickered, the first sign of life since he collapsed. His lips moved and Rebekah leaned close to feel his gasping, warm breath on her ear.

He whispered, "It's true. The boy saved me. But they got away with McKinnon horses and..."

Laramie knelt next to the older man, looking at Rebekah to gauge what he was saying. Rebekah shook her head. "He needs to be still. Questions later."

But Mosby finished with, "...they stole Butler horses, too."

Laramie straightened and stepped back so Rebekah could examine where the bleeding was coming from—square in Mosby's back.

There were few things lower in the territory than a back-shooting horse thief.

Jimmy skidded into the room and to Rebekah's side, setting her bag on the floor next to her. She quickly opened it and pulled out her scissors to begin cutting away Mosby's vest and shirt from the wound. She heard Laramie quietly relaying Mosby's partial report to Doctor McKinnon. It was enough to make Glenn Butler explode.

He railed, "If my horses were stolen, it was the Wallace clan for sure! Everyone knows how they threatened me after I licked them in the cavalry contract. Likely this boy just brought Mosby here to try and look innocent."

The wound was deep. Rebekah pressed a firm hand with gauze over it, instructing Jimmy to tape it in place. Poor Jimmy looked even paler at the sight of so much blood coming from his new friend.

Rebekah stood and said to Steve, "Please take him upstairs to the guest room. Gently. I'll tend him there."

She glanced up in time to see Trey rebuff Glenn Butler's accusation. But he wasn't looking at the man. He was looking at Lilly Butler.

Trey's voice had an edge that could have cut anything it came against. "You don't have to try and look innocent if you are."

CHAPTER 3

Hours later, Rebekah came downstairs again. The McKinnon bunkhouse cook, Stubby Goodman, was keeping watch on the old horse wrangler for the night to see if he pulled through. Mosby was in the guest room across the hall from Rebekah's room and she'd leave her door open tonight.

But she wasn't ready for bed just yet. She had much on her mind about the Butler and Wallace families—especially young Trey Wallace, who seemed so angry with her tonight. He wasn't even born when the feud started.

Rebekah avoided local gossip, but everyone within two hundred miles of Centennial Ridge knew of the Butler and Wallace feud and how it started.

Before the Civil War, Glenn Butler was engaged to a young woman that he and Dean had fought over. They both went off to war and only Dean Wallace returned. He brought news that Glenn Butler was killed in battle.

The young woman was devastated but eventually accepted Dean Wallace's proposal of marriage after Wallace bought Butler's spread for taxes. Nearly a year later, Glenn Butler showed up after recovering from his near-fatal wounds. He was enraged to find that he not only lost his ranch, but his sweetheart was married to his worst enemy and expecting the man's child.

The feud had gone on for decades. It never turned deadly, at least not to public knowledge. Now both Dean Wallace and Glenn Butler were widowers with one child each—Glenn's daughter Lilly and Dean's son Trey.

Rebekah had treated Trey for pneumonia three years ago, and she sensed a different spirit in him from the hardness and anger of his father.

But she hadn't seen the Wallace clan much since. They kept to themselves and wanted to be left alone. Rebekah decided long ago to help those who were willing to accept her help. That was even more of a challenge with her being a female physician. Yet the Wallace family were among those who didn't care as long as she treated them fairly, something few people in the area did.

She still felt bonded with Trey; he was her first patient after she'd been run off the Omaha Indian Reservation, and helped her heal enough to continue her work as a physician in the west.

Rebekah entered the parlor to find Doctor McKinnon standing near the fireplace, staring absently at the cold hearth. A rifle was leaned against it. Jimmy was sprawled in a chair he'd pulled back into the room from where it had been stored for the party, a shotgun in his crossed arms.

Doctor McKinnon turned at her entrance and Jimmy sprang to his feet, laying the shotgun across the arms of the chair. He stared at her, questions filling his eyes but nothing came out. Then he shoved his hands deep in his pockets and swallowed.

"Sorry I wasn't much help with Mr. Mosby, Miss Rebekah," he said quietly.

Rebekah approached Doctor McKinnon, who had poured her a warm cup of tea from a tray.

She accepted it with quiet thanks and took a sip before

addressing Jimmy. "You did well, Just Jimmy. He's resting now and in God's hands."

The words felt strange on her lips after her recent return to her faith. But she believed them with all her heart.

"And as I said earlier, Stubby is like a doctor on the ranch and a most capable assistant. He's set more bones in his lifetime than I have."

Jimmy hung his head. "I could have at least gone after those horse thieves with Mr. Laramie, but he wanted me to stay here and stand guard in case they came back this way."

Rebekah took another sip of tea, the warmth coating her strained throat from the evening's stress. "Laramie is a wise man, and you were wise to heed him. But Jimmy, I'm so sorry your party was spoiled."

Jimmy looked up, his smile faint but there. Few things could keep him down for long. "Aw, it's all right, Miss Rebekah. I had a grand time while it lasted."

Doctor McKinnon picked up the teapot and offered Rebekah a refill. She held her cup out as he said, "Did someone say the celebration was over?"

He nodded to the back corner of the parlor with a twinkle in his eye, reminding Rebekah ever so much why she was grateful to call the McKinnon Ranch "home."

She returned his smile and said with a tone of mischief, "Why, Doctor McKinnon, I didn't mean to indicate it was over completely."

While Jimmy stood dumbfounded, Rebekah headed for the piano situated in the corner by the fireplace. She went around it to the bench and set her tea cup on the closed lid. She seated herself, appreciative that the piano faced the room so she could watch Jimmy's surprised expression as she ran the scales. The touch of ivory felt incredible after probing a bullet from Ol' Mosby's flesh.

It'd been a long time since she played but after a few warm-up strokes, she went into one of Jimmy's favorite hymns.

Blessed assurance, Jesus is mine
Oh what a foretaste of glory divine!

She sang the first few lines, although her voice wobbled from lack of use in singing. She motioned with her head for Doctor McKinnon and Jimmy to join her. They came to stand by the piano and sang out.

Heir of salvation, purchase of God,
Born of his Spirit, washed in his blood.

This is my story, this is my song,
Praising my Savior all the day long;
This is my story, this is my song,
Praising my Savior all the day long.

They sang the other verses, then Rebekah finished the hymn with a flourish of the keys and rested her hands in her lap, smiling at Jimmy.

Jimmy's eyes welled with tears. "That was the best birthday present anyone ever gave me."

Doctor McKinnon scooped a tear from his eye before it dripped, but he was smiling. He cleared the emotion from his throat. "Well, I don't mind playing second fiddle to that, but I do have something I was going give you at the end of the evening, young man."

Doctor McKinnon went to the sideboard and opened a drawer to withdraw a wrapped package. He handed it to Jimmy, who stood shocked. Rebekah wondered when the last time was he'd received a wrapped gift. He didn't seem to know what to do.

She laughed softly and placed an envelope on top of the package. "Open it, Jimmy, along with this."

Jimmy gulped and reverently laid the two pieces side-by-side on the piano. He started with the wrapped package, untying the ribbon and folding back the paper like he planned to reuse it for years to come.

His grin widened when he realized it was a book. "Good gracious, Doc McKinnon. Miss Rebekah has been teaching me to read since we got to the ranch. I'll sure read this a bunch of times once I learn good enough, and I finish reading the Bible."

"I expect no less from you, Jimmy. I'm proud to have you working on my ranch."

Jimmy dipped his head at the compliment and shifted to take up Rebekah's gift. He opened it with the same reverence as the brown wrapping paper, as though he could reuse a sealed envelope. He withdrew the Currier and Ives card, his face glowing as he admired the magnificent racehorses on the front.

"There's more, Jimmy."

He looked puzzled and shook the envelope. Two tickets fell out. He yelped when they fluttered to the floor, and quickly retrieved them, his grin growing again.

"These are to that Donovan Brothers Circus that's coming in a few months, ain't it, Miss Rebekah? I've been saving back some of my pay so that I could get a ticket. Do I need two tickets?"

Rebekah shook her head as she came around the piano beside him. "No, Jimmy, there's one ticket for you and one ticket for you to take a new friend. You may take whomever you wish. But not me, I'm not much for circuses. I know you'll enjoy it though."

Rebekah wrapped him in a side hug and planted a kiss on his cheek. "Happy birthday, Just Jimmy."

She could tell from his bright eyes that he was on the verge of bawling. "Much obliged, Miss Rebekah and Doc McKinnon. This is the best birthday I've ever had."

CHAPTER 4

Fear shot through Rebekah, the blanket covering her mouth and suffocating her. She wrenched it away, gasping.

After blinking several times, her heart slowed along with her breathing. She took in the oak four-poster bed, the handmade quilt clenched in her white knuckled hands, and the soft burgundy drapes barely letting in the early morning sun.

Rebekah was on the McKinnon Ranch, in the bedroom she'd spent summers in as a youth. Her bedroom. Her home.

She was safe.

Warmth flowed through her chilled body and she closed her eyes with one long, deep sigh.

Her days of captivity in the bandit valley were over. How many times did she need to remind herself of that?

Rebekah swung her legs off the bed with a good stretch. Today would be different from the others since her return to McKinnon Ranch. It was time to close the terror and return to her life, to put the past behind and look toward the future. That would start with asking Doctor McKinnon a very important question at breakfast.

Rebekah glanced at the night stand that held her Tiffany lamp with its glass shade—a medical school graduation gift from Doctor McKinnon—and the tintype she always left there for safekeeping. Her recent adventures made her grateful she didn't carry the one photograph she had of her parents.

Rebekah picked up the tintype and traced her fingers over her father's strong jawline. He had been full-blood Omaha and not well educated in the European sense, but he was the strongest, most intelligent man Rebekah had ever known. He pushed her to learn, to be all she could for her people.

Rebekah swallowed tears over her failure, but she wouldn't give up. Her father's eyes, golden brown so like her own she could envision them in the black-and-white image, stared at her and instilled her with ancient courage. With God's help, something he taught her to rely on, she would never give up.

She kissed his face and then the face of her white stepmother whom she had grown to love early in life. She returned the photograph to the nightstand. It was time to take breakfast with Doctor McKinnon, her stepmother's brother, for the first time since her return.

Hopefully she wasn't too late as she'd been the past several mornings after sleeping in, recovering per her doctor's orders. And she still needed to check on her own patient.

A short time later, Rebekah descended the stairs, her hand gliding lightly on the cherrywood railing. The sweet scent of freshly baked cinnamon rolls wafted up to tell her *good morning*.

She smiled. The McKinnon Ranch house cook, Stubby's brother Freddy, normally made cinnamon rolls on Sunday morning. This was Saturday, but it was as though the old man knew she'd be down for breakfast and prepared her favorite.

The dining room was to the left of the grand staircase, opposite the entrance to the parlor. Rebekah spared a glance at the parlor doorway, remembering Trey Wallace standing there, staring down the crowd of people.

A deep voice called to her from the dining room. "Good morning, Becka. How's our patient today?"

Rebekah entered the dining room to see Doctor McKinnon in his place at the head of the white linen covered table. He had a saucer in one hand and tea cup in the other, carefully pouring coffee from the cup to the saucer.

She teased, "I see you still drink coffee your own way."

Rebekah seated herself as he blew on the coffee and took a long sip from the saucer before replying, "You know what it's like for a doctor in the west. You wait for your coffee to cool down and you'll be left drinking a cold cup every time."

"Agreed, although it's not been that way the past few weeks for me, until my new patient arrived. But Mosby is resting well. I'll still keep a close eye on him today."

The swinging door separating the kitchen and the dining room swung open, admitting Freddy Goodman, the ranch house cook. He carried a coffee pot and a cup and saucer.

"Those sweet rolls are coming out of the oven and the icing will melt in a jiffy. Do you want one or three this morning, Miss Becka?"

So few people called her "Becka" besides the McKinnon Ranch folks. It left her off-balance but warm at the same time.

"Considering I've done little but lie around and gain weight since I've been back, let's make it one, shall we? And thank you."

She patted his hand, knowing Freddy would understand that she appreciated his thoughtfulness as well as his cooking.

After Freddy returned to the kitchen, Doctor McKinnon scooted his chair back and went to the buffet where he opened a drawer. He retrieved a cluster of envelopes and brought them to the table, laying them by Rebekah's empty plate.

"I've been saving these for the first morning we took breakfast together. I wanted you to rest up before charging into any kind of business."

Rebekah laid her hand on a stack of mail that came in her

absence, not wanting to look at it until she asked the one question that burned continually in her heart the past three years.

She looked her uncle in the eyes. "Has there been any news?"

Doctor McKinnon broke from her gaze to pour more coffee into his saucer. Then he set it aside without drinking and crossed his arms on the table in front of him, leaning toward her as he spoke in his serious, businessman tone.

"That's something I've been saving to share with you once you were recovered. There is news."

Rebekah held her breath, willing him to speak faster.

"Jeffrey Harris, a newly elected U.S. senator from Wyoming, is willing to help if we renew the fight to get you back on the reservation."

Rebekah closed her eyes, taking a short breath. She took another, a gasp. She felt Doctor McKinnon's warm, calloused hand cover hers. She turned hers over to clasp it as her breathing slowed to normal.

His voice cut through the fog of memories and her pounding heart when he said, "Becka, I don't want you to get your hopes up too high, too fast. Wyoming politics are still in their infancy with statehood being only a few years old. But Harris does have pull here and in Nebraska. He's friends with the governor."

Rebekah opened her eyes, letting out a long breath. She squeezed Doctor McKinnon's hand and released it. The kitchen door swung open and the scrumptious aroma of cinnamon rolls filled her being, marking this moment as a turning point in her life.

Freddy shoveled eggs and bacon onto her plate, then added two large cinnamon rolls. "By my eye—and I know these things, young lady—you could put on a few more pounds after the sorry feedings you got while you were away."

Doctor McKinnon chuckled when Freddy slid two cinnamon rolls on his plate, patting his rotund waistline. "And what is your excuse for putting pounds on me, Freddy?"

Freddy snorted. "Got to keep you fattened up if you go out with the boys for rounding up those horses. That brother of mine poisons those poor hands with his cooking."

Rebekah joined Doctor McKinnon in a light chuckle, regaining her composure as Freddy left.

"Never argue with the cook."

Doctor McKinnon said the same words at the exact same time, leaving them both to laugh heartily. It felt so good to share a conversation with someone who understood her work as a doctor in the west and also her personal battles. She had missed her uncle Robert dearly.

After Doctor McKinnon blessed the food, Rebekah took up a forkful of cinnamon roll with one hand and a portion of the envelope stack with the other. She flipped through the first few before one caught her eye. It was from Mrs. Gladys Haberdasher, who was part of a national women's association.

Rebekah poured coffee into her saucer, took a quick sip and opened the envelope with the silver letter opener that Doctor McKinnon had supplied. She hadn't heard from Mrs. Haberdasher since they communicated about Rebekah's recommendation of Lilly Butler to a law college in Washington, D.C. Mrs. Haberdasher's husband was on the board of the college and instrumental in helping get Lilly's application accepted.

Rebekah unfolded the letter and read quietly to herself while Doctor McKinnon enjoyed his cinnamon rolls. But only a few paragraphs in and Rebekah let out a little gasp. She quickly read the remainder of the letter, letting her fork rest on her plate and her hand come up to rub her temple. She read the first part again.

"Bad news?" Doctor McKinnon asked.

Rebekah lowered the letter. "Very bad, and shocking. Mrs. Haberdasher informed me that Lilly was expelled from school a few weeks before the semester ended."

Doctor McKinnon wiped icing from his lips, his brows knitted together. "That's not what Glenn Butler said."

Rebekah handed the letter to him. "Perhaps lying is a family trait we weren't aware of."

Rebekah watched Doctor McKinnon's reaction to the letter that stated Lilly was expelled for cheating. Mrs. Haberdasher expressed that there was no room in law for someone who did not even have the ethics to earn their degree fairly.

What was most crushing was the last few lines, expressing Mrs. Haberdasher's disappointment that Lilly had been accepted into the school on Rebekah's recommendation.

Doctor McKinnon's frown deepened, causing Rebekah's heart to quicken. He was thinking something she hadn't realized yet.

"What is it, Uncle Robert?"

He laid the letter aside and drank the rest of his cooled coffee before meeting her eyes.

"Mr. Haberdasher is old friends with Senator Jeffrey Harris. They went to that school of law and graduated together."

He paused, and the significance sank into the pit of Rebekah's stomach. He continued, "We need to straighten this out. We have an uphill battle already to get you back on the reservation."

Freddy's delicious cinnamon rolls wouldn't be putting any pounds on Rebekah today. She couldn't eat another bite.

CHAPTER 5

Rebekah drove the buggy on the trip into Centennial Ridge. Jimmy sat beside her, licking his fingers after finishing the last of the cinnamon rolls she brought him. Ahead of them, the frontier town was in view, yet miles away. The westbound train rolled in, white steam drifting from the smokestack after whistling its approach. The train came to a complete stop before the sound of the whistle reached them.

Jimmy smacked his lips. "I can't decide which of those brothers cooks better."

Rebekah glanced over at him. "The way you devoured those, I thought maybe you'd missed breakfast with Stubby."

Jimmy's eyes widened. "Was you wanting one of them rolls? There were only four, so I thought they were all for me."

Rebekah shook her head, realizing how dry her question had sounded. She was preoccupied with the letters in her medical bag, and her morning's mission.

"They were all for you, Just Jimmy. I never want you to be hungry as a growing boy."

Jimmy grinned. "You take awful good care of me, Miss

Rebekah. You're the best friend I've ever had. Who was your best friend before me?"

Rebekah chuckled, then sobered, her heart heavy. "That's a complicated question, Jimmy. But you're certainly one of the best. I wouldn't be alive right now if not for you."

Abruptly, Jimmy threw his arm around her shoulders and gave her a hard squeeze, jerking her neck and almost undoing the part about saving her life.

He released her and took up the reins. "I'll drive the rest of the way, you just sit back and relax. I hardly ever see you doing that. Besides, you look like you got a lot on your mind."

Rebekah sighed, her empty hands fidgeting in her lap. "I do need to straighten something out, and I appreciate you driving me into town."

Jimmy shrugged, grinning sheepishly. "I reckon after falling asleep in the parlor and getting up too late to join the boys out branding, Laramie figured it best I just stayed close to the house and do whatever you and Doc McKinnon needed. Mr. Laramie sure is a good man."

Rebekah gazed out at the dull sagebrush the color of zinc interrupting the tall, lush prairie grasses. Cottonwoods and willow thickets punctuated the terrain leading to the foothills of the Medicine Bow Mountains. Such a beautiful landscape, lost to her forever if not for Laramie Jones.

She answered quietly, "He is."

Jimmy cleared his throat. "Mind if I ask you something, Miss Rebekah?"

She hoped it wasn't about Laramie, but she nodded, gaze still on the countryside, one hand resting on the iron bar of the buggy awning.

Jimmy continued, "I was thinking about Miss Lilly Butler."

Rebekah turned to him with a raised eyebrow.

His face reddened and he quickly shook his head. "Nothing like that, ma'am. I'm just wondering if you know if she's a Christian lady? The reason being, from what I've heard from Steve—he's awful sweet on her—she's mighty angry at Dean Wallace for cheating her daddy out of his land back before she was born, and she grew up poorer because her daddy had to start over. I mean, she ain't got to forget what Wallace done, but staying mad about it is hurting her more. She seems like a tore up girl to me, and forgiving would get her to healing."

Rebekah returned her gaze to the prairie and a clump of cottonwoods they were passing, then round the green hillside, soaking in the lushness of Wyoming territory so different from the Chihuahuan Desert that Sancho Guerra dragged her across as a captive...

Rebekah clenched the buggy awning, hot anger roiling inside her, but she refused to acknowledge it. She wouldn't be a person of anger or bitterness.

"Forgiveness isn't that simple, Jimmy."

They drove in silence as Rebekah thought of the Guerras. Her own words betrayed her. But the Guerras were all dead. Why did she need to forgive them?

Jimmy finally broke the silence. "I beg to differ, Miss Rebekah. Forgiveness is simple. It's just not easy."

CHAPTER 6

R ebekah and Jimmy only accomplished half their mission. She did mail her letters, asking for details from Mrs. Haberdasher and Lilly's school records. But neither Glenn Butler nor Lilly were at their house outside Centennial Ridge. Their ranch adjoined the town and Glenn Butler, being an aspiring socialite, had built the house to be a short drive from any events.

Rebekah and Jimmy did encounter Steve who was in town picking up a wagon load of goods with another ranch hand. They needed traveling supplies for their next attempt at hunting down the stolen McKinnon horses.

Steve sent the other hand back to the ranch, saying he would see that Miss Rebekah returned safe and sound. It wasn't necessary, but Rebekah suspected Steve wanted to hang around as long as he could. She wasn't the only one hoping to see Lilly Butler.

But after they finished shopping and checked the house once again, the family hadn't returned. Rebekah gave up, deciding she would have to speak with Lilly tomorrow at church.

Church.

This would be Rebekah's first time darkening the doors of the Centennial Ridge church in years.

The trio headed out of town, Steve trotting alongside the buggy on his sorrel gelding. He was a good-looking young man at twenty-three, hardworking, always making those around him laugh and the long days pass easier. He was said to be the best horse wrangler on the ranch, second only to Ol' Mosby.

While Rebekah wouldn't say Steve was a match for Lilly Butler, she did hope he found a good woman to settle down with someday.

They neared the entrance of the McKinnon Ranch where home lay five miles beyond. The entrance was guarded on one side with a tumble of boulders that had slid down ages ago from the foothills and now boasted a spray of pines and cottonwoods that laid claim to the earth between the rocks. The foothills to the west paraded out to the Medicine Bow Mountains.

Jimmy flicked the reins on the buggy horse to encourage her through the overhang with its iron sign hanging down, the *MKR* brand.

But right before passing under it, Jimmy yanked back on the reins, causing the buggy horse to toss her head in protest. Jimmy didn't normally jerk a bit in a horse's mouth, and that alerted Rebekah more than the way his shoulders stiffened. He sat up straight and looked toward the foothills.

Steve, who had outridden them through the gate, pulled up and swung his sorrel around. He scowled, something the normally congenial, happy-go-lucky Steve didn't do.

"What do you think you're doing, Jimmy?"

Rebekah was surprised at the way Steve barked at Jimmy. Had the two gotten into a scrap?

Jimmy partly turned in the buggy seat, blocking Rebekah's view of the foothills. "There's some fellows hunkered down in those rocks above the valley."

Steve turned in the saddle, squinting. Rebekah slid forward on the buggy seat and peered around Jimmy's shoulder. She saw nothing but a cacophony of sage brush, cottonwoods, and a stand of young pines that had not survived the last winter. They were fallen over, piled as if lumberjacks on a drunken rage had slayed them.

Jimmy stretched out his long arm, slender finger pointing at the dead pines. "Right in there. It's a kind of pocket where you can see the whole valley. There! Just to the left. I make out four or five horses, saddled and tied up in the brush."

Steve put his hand on his hip over his six-gun, this time squinting at Jimmy. "I don't see nothing—"

Rebekah grabbed Jimmy's arm. "I see them. One moved out of the shadows and the sun reflected off his rifle barrel."

Jimmy nodded. "I seen it, too."

Steve glanced back. "What would men with rifles be doing there? Ain't no good hunting this time of day. Besides, they're on McKinnon land."

Rebekah reached around Jimmy to take the reins from his loose hands. "I suggest we find out."

Both Jimmy and Steve looked at her as if to object. Doctor McKinnon and Laramie Jones had given strict orders to all the ranch hands that Miss Rebekah was to be protected at all cost. But these young men also knew better than to try to take the reins out of her hands.

Rebekah turned the buggy horse's nose toward a trail that led up to the top of the first foothill. From there, they would be higher than the men who were just above the valley.

The trail wasn't much of one. Halfway up, Rebekah announced they needed to abandon the buggy and take the rest of the way on foot. She urged Steve to keep going on his sorrel and get a look at what those men were doing.

She took her medical bag and hiked her skirts above her ankles as she climbed the trail. Jimmy held her elbow to support her in case she slipped on the loose gravel of the hill that could justifiably be called a mountain.

By the time they caught up with Steve, he had dismounted and was pressed against the base of a one-hundred-foot pine, his Winchester '73 tucked under his arm as he scanned the dead pine cluster. His scowl deepened into a concerned frown.

"Miss Becka, those fellows are nestled in there like they plan to ambush someone. They..."

Steve's voice trailed as Rebekah held a finger to her lips. She knew the echo in the foothills could carry their voices to the men below. She moved a step forward, getting a better look up the northern trail leading into the valley.

A lone horse and rider were trotting into the open country, heading for the road leading to the McKinnon ranch house.

The men among the rocks shifted and she could see them shouldering their rifles and aiming at the man in the valley floor. Steve was right. It was an ambush.

Steve took aim, his rifle shouldered. He fired a shot at the backside of the dead pines. At the same time, Jimmy drew his six gun and pulled Rebekah to the shelter of a boulder.

Startled by the rifle shot from behind them, the four men swung around and one fired back, but two others ran for their horses. Steve fired again, striking the ground between them and their mounts, causing them to skitter back.

Steve fired off a couple more shots. Rebekah peered around the boulder to see the man in the valley had taken off at a gallop back the way he came from, hunched low over the saddle, the only protection he had in the open space.

But the men below had their own troubles. Steve fired again, letting them know if they poked their heads above the fallen pines, he could pluck them off like turkeys.

Steve hollered, "How's it feel, getting ambushed, you low-down cowards!"

Silence fell over the valley. Then Steve stiffened, shock marking his face.

Rebekah asked, "Who are those men? Can you make them out?"

Rebekah detected the hesitation in Steve's voice when he answered, "Yes, ma'am. They're from Glenn Butler's outfit."

Rebekah slid her hand up the rock so that she could stand pressed against it as she peered around. It looked like the men were crawling toward their horses and Steve was letting them go.

"Why would Glenn Butler's men be ambushing a McKinnon ranch hand?"

Steve still sounded hesitant as he answered, "They weren't shooting at one of our men, ma'am. That rider in the valley, I recognized his horse. It was Trey Wallace."

CHAPTER 7

The Sunday morning service was packed. Parishioners from all walks of life filled the church, a sanctuary from the struggles and hardships of western life. They sang loud and listened close to the admonitions of Pastor Richard Wharton.

Rebekah sat on the fourth pew from the front on the right-hand side, squished between Doctor McKinnon and Jimmy. The McKinnon crew, at least the ones who attended church, took up two long pews.

Rebekah felt shoehorned in. She wanted to be attentive to the service, but really, she spent most of it observing two other ranch crews that had their designated sections.

Glenn Butler and Lilly occupied the front row to the right with their ranch foreman and a few other hands. Rebekah didn't recognize any of them as the ones who had tried to ambush Trey Wallace. She doubted those men would show their faces for a while.

On the front row to the left was Trey Wallace, his father Dean, and six men from their crew. One thing marked both the Butler and Wallace men—they all openly wore their six guns.

Rebekah could sense Jimmy's split attention between watching the feuding families on the front rows and paying attention to the sermon. He was a devout boy, yet ready to spring into action to defend the weak.

When Pastor Wharton called for prayer, Rebekah quickly bowed her head and closed her eyes, ashamed she hadn't paid more attention to the sermon. Her mind was on speaking with Lilly right after the *amen*.

There was a ripple of tension as most the parishioners stood and slowly gathered their things. Rebekah noticed one mother with hands on her children's shoulders, holding them back.

People casually shuffled in place while they waited for Glenn Butler to rise and strut out of the church like it was his private sanctuary. His crew followed. Rebekah tried to catch Lilly's gaze, but the young woman kept her head down.

The Wallace crew stood at the same time, lined up like soldiers ready to enter battle. The cowboys rested their hands on the butts of their six-guns, staring down the Butlers leaving the church.

Dean Wallace swept his gaze around the congregation and suddenly, everyone was in a great hurry to leave.

Amidst the shuffle, Dean Wallace's eyes landed on Rebekah. They held the same look of disgust as Trey's had the night he brought in Mosby. Except Dean Wallace's gaze was far more intense, embittered; filled with decades of hate and anger.

Rebekah felt the urge to move and quickly followed Doctor McKinnon out. She noticed Steve had already slipped ahead in the crowd that was filing slowly out the door as they shook Pastor Wharton's hand.

Doctor McKinnon greeted the preacher with a hearty handshake and a few words. Then Pastor Wharton turned to Rebekah, hand out, a grim smile on his face. "Doctor Rebekah LaRoche. It's been a long time."

Of the McKinnon crew behind her, only Laramie Jones would

know what Pastor Wharton meant. It wasn't that she'd been traveling for quite a while since her last visit to the ranch.

Rebekah took his hand to shake, fully expecting to be admonished for her long absence, and her lack of attention during the service.

But Pastor Wharton's smile lightened and he shook her hand firmly.

"Welcome back."

The simple words caused tears to spring into Rebekah's eyes and she swallowed. It was unlike her to lose her composure in public, but in that moment, she could hardly piece herself together. A word from her Native tongue slipped out. "*Hó.* That is, thank you."

Pastor Wharton was one of few people in the area who knew her heritage and background. More importantly, he accepted it.

Doctor McKinnon imparted sage words to her long ago: being a mediocre doctor was tragic, but keep away from a mediocre man of God. Pastor Wharton was certainly not that.

Rebekah went down the steps of the church, taking Doctor McKinnon's hand on the last few. She looked around and spotted Glenn Butler helping Lilly into their carriage. Though their home was only a short walk from town, Glenn Butler never missed an opportunity to display his fine buggy with its black fringed canopy.

Rebekah mumbled an, "excuse me," to Doctor McKinnon and hurried toward the buggy. She wasn't the only one who had visiting the Butlers in mind.

Steve was already there, holding the horse's head in an attempt to speak with Lilly on the other side as she got into the buggy. Doctor McKinnon and Laramie Jones were right behind Rebekah.

Glenn Butler grabbed the buggy seat and started to hoist himself aboard when Rebekah tapped his shoulder. "Mr. Butler, I need to speak with Lilly a moment, please."

Glenn Butler looked back, one hand still on the buggy arm. "We're in a hurry, Doctor LaRoche."

Laramie flanked Rebekah, his dark brown Sunday suit coat unbuttoned, allowing a hint of the six-gun he wore to show. His tone was low and serious. "Got plans to ambush the Wallaces today?"

Glenn Butler released the buggy seat and squared off with Laramie Jones. Though Glenn Butler faced Laramie, he spoke to Doctor McKinnon.

"Robert, you better tell your hired hand to bridle his tongue and not be throwing around false accusations about one of the most powerful men in this territory. I don't take kindly to it."

Doctor McKinnon flipped his own coat back and tucked his thumbs in his vest pockets, the posture he assumed when conducting a serious negotiation with someone he considered a friend.

"Glenn, two of my men caught some of your crew about to ambush young Wallace on my land yesterday. I hoped you could tell us what happened."

Glenn Butler's gaze swept beyond Rebekah and she realized Jimmy stood behind her shoulder. Then he swung around to include Steve, who still held the buggy horse's head.

"Two of your *men*, or two of your *boys*?"

Steve immediately released his hold on the horse's bridle and came at Glenn Butler, eyes firing hot lead.

Laramie Jones put out an arm to block Steve's advance. "Mr. Butler, these so-called *boys* could have shot your *men* to pieces yesterday. Now, are you denying you sent those hands out to murder Trey Wallace?"

The accusation hung heavy in the air like a low thunderhead.

Glenn Butler let his eyes roam the McKinnon crew despite a disturbance not a dozen yards away. The Wallaces had mounted and were trotting their horses toward them. Rebekah gave them a glance as they passed within inches of Glenn Butler's agitated buggy horse.

The animal took a few steps back, eliciting a gasp from Lilly Butler as she held onto the seat. Steve quickly took the horse's head again.

Rebekah didn't miss the hard glare that Trey Wallace sent the young woman. They held each other's gaze a moment as he passed, then he kicked his horse to catch up with his father as the Wallace crew galloped away from the church. The Wallaces weren't regular church-goers and Rebekah had a feeling it wasn't for the sermon that they'd come that morning.

Glenn Butler watched them ride away, then slowly turned back to Laramie. "I should have you arrested for slander. But I'm going to let it go, just this once. As long as the McKinnon *boys* stay away from my men."

Glenn Butler boarded the buggy and grabbed the reins. Rebekah pushed forward to put her hand on the buggy arm.

She spoke past him and to Lilly, who finally met her eyes. "Lilly, I need to speak with you. It's urgent. I'll walk you home after—"

"She has nothing to say to you." Glenn Butler slapped the reins across the back of the buggy horse, shooting the animal into an immediate trot. Rebekah lost her grip on the buggy seat and took a stumbling step, trying to maintain her balance.

Laramie steadied her as he said, "That Glenn Butler is about to show everyone in the valley who he really is—a polecat in a suit."

Doctor McKinnon slipped his arm around Rebekah and gave her a light squeeze. "Don't worry, Becka. We'll get things straightened out."

Only he knew how important it was for her to speak with Lilly Butler. But she had a feeling Laramie was right. Everyone in the valley would soon know who Glenn Butler truly was.

CHAPTER 8

Rebekah settled against the trunk of a weeping willow by the lake downhill from the church. Taking advantage of the beautiful summer day, most of the church parishioners opted for a picnic under the willows. Children splashed on the banks while young people rowed out in boats to fish and tease one another.

Rebekah had eaten lightly and sought out this willow away from the crowd. It leaned uphill, forming a perfect seat for her to settle at the root base of the young tree, and enjoy its mix of sunshine and shade.

She closed her eyes. Despite Glenn and Lilly Butler's abrupt departure and the threat hanging over Rebekah due to them, she hadn't felt this rested and at peace since... since when?

"Good spot you've got here."

Rebekah jolted to one side away from the voice, her hands planted on the ground beneath her, ready to spring away, away from danger. It took her a moment to realize there wasn't any.

Laramie Jones—Lee—was hunkered down next to her. He winced. "Didn't mean to startle you, Becka, thought you heard me come up. We must be getting old."

He winced again, scrubbing a hand over his mouth to hide a grimace.

Rebekah felt a girlish urge to stick her tongue out at him. "Speak for yourself, *old* Laramie Jones."

"Oh, I know I'm aging when I have boys like that Jimmy work circles around me every day. I figure to have a few good years left in me, though."

Rebekah smiled, casting a glance at the lake where Jimmy was in a boat with two younger boys. The way he waved his hands and talked, she wouldn't doubt he was preaching them a second sermon.

"He's a good boy."

Heaviness settled over Rebekah's heart, that thundercloud covering her despite her wish to be free from it forever.

"If it weren't for him, and Fernando Contrera, and you, I wouldn't be here." She met Lee's eyes. "I really don't think I could ever thank you enough for saving me from that valley of death."

Rebekah felt control on her emotions slipping again. Her tight grip on her composure that she maintained most of her life was cracking. What had the Guerras done to her?

Lee didn't say anything, just watched her for several moments as she stared at the sparkling waters. She finally asked in a whisper, "Do you think God allowed me to go through that to bring me to my knees?"

Lee shifted from his squatted position to sit next to her, stretching one long leg out and propping his arm on his bent knee. "No, Becka, I don't. But He'll sure meet you there every time."

Rebekah tried to swallow, but her throat was too tight. She reached up a hand to massage it, the feel of Sancho Guerra's powerful fingers clamped around her throat, choking the life from her. When would she feel free of that, of him? If only she could strike back, to release the anger and fear and pain for good.

She realized her eyes were squeezed shut and she quickly

popped them open to take in the sereneness of the lake and the presence of those who cared for her.

"I don't know if I can forgive them."

"You can't on your own."

Rebekah was startled, realizing she spoke the words out loud and that Lee answered. He went on. "Those Guerras got their comeuppance. Everyone does, eventually. Why should you keep suffering? God can give you the strength to forgive even them."

She picked at lint on her skirt. "You're right as always, my friend. My old, *old* friend." She tried to sound teasing, but the thundercloud heaviness was on her tongue, too.

Lee chuckled. "We've been through a lot, both together and apart. Doctor McKinnon told me about Senator Harris' offer... and what happened with Lilly Butler. I'll sure help with what's going on, best I can."

Rebekah pinched the fabric of her dress between her thumb and forefinger. The contentment she felt moments ago was fleeting. The reality of her life didn't allow much time for rest or peace. If only she could find a way to capture it and hold it in her heart no matter what the storms were around her.

"I cannot let anything restrain me from going back to the reservation," she said. "From going home."

Rebekah's fingers twisted her skirt in a death grip and she fought to hold in her fears.

Lee covered her hand, squeezing it. She released her grip with a shaky sigh and let him hold her hand loosely in his. She had to stop holding so tightly to the things she wanted. She had to learn to let go, even if it meant letting go of her heart's desires.

"Becka, I don't know if God will make a way for you to return to the reservation, but I do know He has a home for you right here. You know that, don't you?"

Rebekah nodded, fighting to keep her hands loose, to not clench them. "Lee, have you ever threatened God?"

Silence. If he had, it wasn't something he was ready to admit.

Rebekah went on. "I did, when I was facing that hearing to have me banned from practicing medicine on the reservation because of what happened with Agent Graham's wife and daughter. Before my testimony, I told God that if He didn't allow me to stay on the reservation, I would no longer believe in Him, no longer follow Him as my father taught me."

Rebekah closed her eyes and squeezed Lee's hand. She needed something to hold onto and this felt right.

"What a foolish thing to say, when what I needed most was a father."

Lee squeezed her hand with that brotherly affection he never failed to show her. He was like no other friend she could imagine having.

His voice was soft and low when he said, "God has forgiven all that, Becka. That's what fathers do."

Rebekah bit her lip and nodded, determined not to weep in public. She could do that in her room later with her Bible and the photograph of her earthly father.

She drew in a shaky breath. It was time to move away from personal feelings.

"If you can spare him, I'd like to take Jimmy with me tomorrow to visit the Wallace family," she said. "I feel that whatever happened with Lilly at school, it's tied to the feud. There are always two sides to every story."

Lee was quiet a moment, then said, "I can spare Jimmy for you."

CHAPTER 9

The road to the Wallace ranch wasn't a well-worn path. The clan scarcely left their home and no one visited them. It was like Trey indicated when he barged in on Jimmy's party to save Mosby's life—people regarded the Wallace family as outcasts. He wasn't wrong, with the exception of Doctor McKinnon. Rebekah had considered herself unbiased as well.

But she hadn't been unbiased when she wrote the recommendation letter for Lilly Butler. Maybe she should have spent a little more time understanding the root of the feud before she seemingly took a side.

That morning, she had tended Mosby and changed the bandage on his wound while he told her how young Wallace risked his life to get between Mosby and the horse rustlers. And that was after Mosby had thought Trey was one of the rustlers and nearly shot him.

He'd seen Trey turning bad a few years before, walking the path his father took that drove Mosby away from working for the Wallace outfit.

"But that boy has some goodness in him, deep down," Ol' Mosby told her.

Rebekah needed to find that goodness.

She and Jimmy rode side-by-side on the road to the Wallace ranch house. Jimmy talked nonstop about the pastor's sermon, the new people he met at church the day before, and the fruitless search for the horse rustlers who nearly killed Mosby.

While she appreciated his protection—neither Doctor McKinnon nor Lee would have allowed her to ride out on her own—she really didn't mind his chatter, either. Tall tales and talking about the world around him were a part of Jimmy, though she also wouldn't mind if he shared details about his past and growing up years.

At sixteen, there couldn't be too much there, yet Jimmy always dodged direct questions she asked him. But that was all right. She hadn't been entirely forthcoming with him either.

All in good time.

Jimmy held the reins loose over his horse's neck in one hand and shoved his hat off to let it dangle down his back, held by a new horsehair stampede string. He used his sleeve to wipe dust and sweat from his forehead.

"You all right, ma'am? I don't mind talking to the wind, been doing that all my life, but I sure don't want it getting you down."

Rebekah shifted in the saddle, making sure her skirts were tucked modestly low on her legs as she rode astride. She never quite mastered sidesaddle, and too often found herself needing to ride astride anyway.

"I'm sorry I've been inattentive, Jimmy. My mind is elsewhere. It's very important I get some things straightened out before Doctor McKinnon and I meet with Senator Jeffrey Harris this week."

Jimmy nodded vigorously. "Mr. Laramie said you're making a trip to Cheyenne. Boy, I'd like to see that capitol building there. But I'll be needed at the ranch if we haven't caught those rustlers by then."

Rebekah nodded absently and Jimmy continued. "I was just

asking because I noticed after church, you and Mr. Laramie were having an awful serious talk. You looked sad, Miss Rebekah. Anything I can do?"

She took a cleansing breath. "You're doing it now, accompanying me to the Wallace ranch. Laramie...he helped me talk other things through."

Jimmy's eyes filled with respect. "That Laramie Jones is a real gentleman, ain't he?"

Rebekah's gaze landed on the Wallace home ahead. "Yes, he's a gentle...man."

Not like the ones they were about to encounter.

In the dusty barnyard between the corral and the ranch-style house that Glenn Butler built before the war—one that Dean Wallace bought for pennies on the dollar—two men stood arguing.

Rebekah recognized Dean Wallace in his fixed stance and mature waistline. Trey stood in front of his father, facing him as he whipped his hat off and slap it against his leg.

"You do that, Pa, and you prove everything they say about us is true!"

Rebekah could see the coil in Dean Wallace's shoulder muscles even as she urged her horse up to a trot. She wasn't in time.

Dean Wallace swung his fist, catching Trey soundly in the jaw. A crack like a branch snapping in an ice storm resounded and Trey staggered. He landed on his backside with a moan.

Rebekah circled them and dismounted under Dean Wallace's glare.

"What're you doing here, woman?"

Rebekah unhooked her medical bag and handed off her reins to Jimmy, who also dismounted. His gaze darted between the barn and house as though watching for an ambush. A wise young man.

Rebekah knelt in the dust beside Trey, who propped himself

on one elbow while he held his jaw. Rebekah spoke to Dean Wallace. "I hate to see what you do to your worst enemy."

Dean Wallace gritted his teeth. "Trey's my son. I hit him harder."

Rebekah put a hand on the young man's shoulder, staring up at the imposing frame of his father.

"That's one way to get him to look up to you."

Rebekah set her bag down and used both hands to run along Trey's jawline. Nothing seemed broken, but he didn't allow further examination. He pulled away and pushed himself to his feet, working his jaw back-and-forth, then it hitched and locked.

Rebekah stood and met his eyes, wanting him to remember the time when she nursed him back to health. There was no appreciation in his eyes, only that same disgust he had shown her at Jimmy's party.

Dean Wallace snapped, "If we need a doctor around here, I'll send for one. Now you get out, you Butler lover."

Rebekah left her bag in the dust. She wasn't finished. "I have my own reasons for mistrusting Glenn Butler, and I need answers about what's going on with young Lilly."

Rebekah flicked her eyes toward Trey, wanting to judge his reaction. He and Lilly were about the same age, and carried on the same feud as their fathers.

But there was a momentary softness in Trey's eyes before they hardened back over. He swiped his hat from the ground and knocked dust from it against his leg, his mouth open slightly from his frozen jaw.

Rebekah wished she could finish examining it, get it back into place. But Dean Wallace had taken note of his son's reaction about Lilly. He grabbed Trey's shirt collar, yanking him to face him.

"Something been going on between you and Butler's daughter again?"

Trey's eyes widened and Rebekah quickly stepped in. "I wasn't indicating anything like that, Mr. Wallace, I just want to know—"

Dean Wallace shot a finger at Rebekah's nose. "As for you, Indian woman, get off my land. Now!"

Rebekah was convinced Trey had answers she needed, but she wouldn't get them today. She hooked her medical bag on her saddle again and swung aboard. Jimmy handed her the reins, his face pale and eyes bulging. Had Dean Wallace frightened him that much?

They rode away at a steady trot. Once out of sight of the house, Rebekah slowed their pace. "Are you all right, Jimmy?"

Jimmy looked at her from the corner of his eye, stiff-necked. "I sure hope I haven't said anything bad, Miss Rebekah. I'm awful sorry if I did."

Rebekah shifted in the saddle to face him. "Why, Jimmy, what are you talking about? You didn't say a word."

Jimmy rubbed the split reins between his gloved thumb, still not meeting her eyes. "I didn't know, ma'am. I always thought... I don't know, I reckoned you were...what with your last name and all, that you had some kind of fancy European ancestors..."

"What you're saying is, you didn't realize I was Omaha Indian until Dean Wallace said what he did?"

He dropped his eyes, and tugged his horse to a stop.

Rebekah's heart sank as she halted her horse. Surely Jimmy wouldn't hold her Indian heritage against her?

Not Jimmy! She couldn't bear that.

Jimmy finally raised his gaze and met her eyes, his own rimmed red. "Sometimes I tell stories, stories I had read to me from dime novels, about the noble Redman and scalping savages. I sure hope I haven't said anything that hurt you, Miss Rebekah. Please forgive me if I did. I'd rather chew barbed wire than hurt you."

Rebekah bit her lip, not sure whether to laugh or cry. She reached over and patted Jimmy's cheek.

"You've never done anything of the sort, young man. You are a kind soul. Please don't ever change."

Jimmy drew in a deep breath and let it out in one long *whish*, his eyes clearing.

"I'll sure try not to, ma'am. But only God could do something good with someone like me."

Rebekah opened her mouth, wanting to broach the subject of Jimmy's past; who he was, how he had really grown up—even as he was still growing up—but she felt in her spirit that this wasn't the time. They'd borne enough revelations for one day.

CHAPTER 10

Cheyenne, state capitol of Wyoming, was no Washington, D.C., but it was just as intimidating and there was as much at stake for Rebekah as when she visited the U.S. capital years ago. But she hadn't been alone in the fight then, and she wasn't alone now.

Doctor McKinnon handed her down from the rented carriage in front of the three-story mansion of the governor, its eggshell-blue shingled façades standing out in the late summer evening sun. Together, she and her uncle would face the gala—and the evening with Senator Jeffrey Harris.

At least part of an evening, and one they had to share with hundreds of others. As a prominent citizen in Wyoming, Doctor McKinnon was among many who received an invitation to the governor's ball held on this chilly, stately evening.

Rebekah wore a new gown, a ready-made one she purchased in Cheyenne. They came two days early on the Union Pacific Railroad for shopping, and in hopes of meeting with Senator Harris before the gala event. In truth, she knew Doctor McKinnon wanted her to have plenty of time to rest after the train ride. Rebekah didn't argue with her doctor's orders. She tired more quickly since her arduous journey in Mexico.

But the senator's packed schedule didn't allow for an earlier meeting. His assistant told them Senator Harris was looking forward to speaking with them that evening.

Rebekah took Doctor McKinnon's arm, observing his aging but handsome face and tuxedo with its lavender satin pocket square that matched her dress. "I don't know what this evening will mean for me, but I couldn't have a more debonair escort."

Doctor McKinnon chuckled and patted her hand. "And I will be the most envied old man in the room."

Rebekah tucked close to her uncle Robert, absently placing her free hand over the flutters in her stomach. Every time she entered a new social situation, whether at the Woman's Medical College of Pennsylvania or New York summers where she worked while attending school, she always wondered how she would fit in, how people would respond to her "swarthy" skin and distinct Omaha features.

Like Jimmy, some people thought she was European—Spanish or Italian. But because of her reputation, most knew where she came from. She'd met a lot of good people in her life. A lot of bad ones, too. What did this western gala hold? More importantly, how would Senator Harris receive her?

Doctor McKinnon showed their invitations at the door and the footman took their wraps. Though summertime, the evenings were chilly in Wyoming, foreshadowing the freezing winds and blistering blizzards that winter held in store.

From the foyer, they entered the ballroom where they found themselves on a platform overlooking a majestic room filled with mahogany woodwork and formal gowns.

The governor and his wife were at the top of the landing, greeting guests as they arrived. Rebekah smiled at the couple, home folks she had known from their visits at Doctor McKinnon's ranch. Her uncle had hosted nearly every family in the state, or so it seemed to her. He was an open and generous man, and Rebekah couldn't have prayed for a better ally to have at her side.

After small talk, they moved on to allow others their chance to greet the governor. Doctor McKinnon angled her toward a group of well-dressed men, one of whom was waving him over. Introductions made, Rebekah took note that none of them were Senator Jeffrey Harris. But the evening was young and she patiently stayed at Doctor McKinnon's side while he visited with friends and business acquaintances.

There was still no sign of Senator Harris as the evening wore on. Rebekah accepted dances from every eligible bachelor in the room ages 18 to 62, but still, the man she wanted to see had yet to make an appearance.

She was dancing the final waltz with Doctor McKinnon when he halted and nodded over her shoulder. Rebekah glanced back to see a young man at the edge of the dance floor, beckoning to them. It was Senator Harris's assistant, Stanley Cook.

Doctor McKinnon escorted her toward him, leaning over to whisper, "It's all right, Becka. We will face this side by side."

Rebekah's mouth was dry and she imagined her face showed the distress that suddenly overcame her. This was the chance she'd longed for—prayed for—to have an audience with someone who had the influence she needed to return to her homeland.

Above the music, Stanley Cook quickly explained that Senator Harris had been delayed but now wanted to meet with them in the library.

The hallway outside the ballroom held a far more serious tone than the gaiety inside. Here, men smoked expensive cigars and plotted their next political or business moves. Cattle kings talked with state representatives, and deals were likely being made.

Was Rebekah imitating them? But whatever those men were concocting, she knew this: hers was a righteous cause, what her father would have encouraged her to fight for with all her heart.

Stanley Cook opened the door to the library, and the sweet musty smell of books welcomed Rebekah in.

Not so welcoming was the man who stood by a moonlit window, puffing on a cigar like it was the last one he owned. He cast a long, slender shadow animated by the way he pulled his hand from his pocket, put it back again, then out once more.

He yanked the cigar from his mouth and waved his hand broadly, dismissing his assistant who left, closing the door with a click. To Rebekah, it sounded like a jailer closing a cell door.

She held tight to Doctor McKinnon's arm as her uncle nodded a greeting. "Jeffrey, it's good to see you. This is my niece, Doctor Rebekah LaRoche."

Senator Harris jerked his head by way of greeting. "I'm familiar with you by reputation, Doc Beck."

His tone wasn't encouraging. Rebekah released Doctor McKinnon's arm and stepped forward, offering her hand to shake. "Thank you for meeting with us, Senator Harris, and your offer to help reinstate me to my people who so desperately need another physician."

Senator Harris stuffed the cigar between his teeth and shook her hand stoutly. At least he wasn't the kind of man who was afraid to meet a woman as an equal.

There wasn't anything she disliked about Senator Harris upon finally meeting him, but she recognized the challenge in his eyes.

"That remains to be seen, Doctor," he said. "I've just had a disturbing visit from one of the leading citizens of Centennial Ridge."

Rebekah's eyebrows furrowed, matching Doctor McKinnon's as he pocketed his hands, rocking back-and-forth on his heels. "I don't understand, Jeffrey."

Senator Harris spoke around the cigar in his mouth. "Mr. Glenn Butler paid me a call this evening. He said that you, Doctor LaRoche, are taking the side of a rogue rancher who has stolen a great many assets from people in the area, including himself and even Doctor McKinnon recently. Something about horse herds and army contracts and a feud that goes back to the War."

With each word he punched out, Rebekah's stomach sank. Shock caused her hands to shake and she gripped them together as her shock turned to anger. How dare Glenn Butler interfere with her life!

Rebekah should have never gotten involved with Lilly Butler's education journey. But as she visualized the young woman's intelligent yet worried look at Jimmy's party, Rebekah could feel no true remorse at helping her.

Doctor McKinnon's voice came through her thoughts and she realized he was explaining to Senator Harris that Rebekah had done no such thing and that Glenn Butler needed to mind his own business.

Rebekah cleared her throat, halting Doctor McKinnon's defense of her. From what she understood, Jeffrey Harris and Robert McKinnon's long-time relationship was sometimes amiable, sometimes not. History was complicated that way.

Rebekah released her hands and spoke in a professional tone. "There has been a misunderstanding, Senator Harris, and it goes back beyond my involvement with the Butlers and the Wallaces. But I can assure you, their feud will not impact my ability to serve on the Omaha Indian Reservation."

Senator Harris leveled his gaze on her. "Butler struck me as a man full of his own ideas about right and wrong. I don't care about his opinion, but the public does. And I care about what the public thinks. I have to or I'll be out of office next term, which is something none of us in this room want."

He pulled the cigar from his mouth and held it between two fingers that he pointed at Rebekah. "Doc Beck, I'm taking a big chance on you with the controversies already surrounding your past reputation on that Indian reservation. If you want my help, stay away from trouble, or you'll be on your own again."

CHAPTER 11

Shouting on the front porch caught Rebekah's attention as she finished changing the dressing on Mosby's wound. It was healing well, no sign of infection, and she was about to tell him he'd be right as rain soon, when the loud voices interrupted.

She raised her eyebrows and Mosby told her to get on and see what the ruckus was about.

Rebekah hurried down the stairs and out the front door, Freddy on her heels. Doctor McKinnon followed, coming out of his study located down the hall. Rebekah stepped onto the front porch to see two young men at the bottom of the steps, shouting at each other.

It was Jimmy and Trey Wallace, who held the reins of his horse gripped in one hand.

Rebekah called above the racket, "Mercy, what is going on here?"

They immediately stopped. Trey glared at her while Jimmy turned, shamefaced.

"I'm sorry, Doc. I seen this fellow riding up and I came and asked what he was doing here, and he started hollering at me. I guess I hollered back some."

Rebekah crossed her arms. "I guess you did."

Beyond the scowl on Trey's face, she saw his swollen jaw and the split at the corner of his lip where his father had hit him. He hadn't thanked her for interfering and it didn't look like that was the reason he'd come today.

Freddy went back inside, mumbling about not having time for fool boys. Doctor McKinnon came to Rebekah's side as he addressed Trey.

"Something we can do for you, young man?"

She could hear the caution in her uncle's voice. They were both mindful of Senator Harris's warning at the gala two days before. Rebekah intended to go into Centennial Ridge that day and sit on Glenn Butler's porch until she had a chance to speak with Lilly.

One thing she didn't need was an angry Trey Wallace on her doorstep.

He shifted his jaw as if trying to get it to work well enough to speak. "I come to see how Ol' Mosby's doing. Same as I tried the other day before your fellows and the Butlers ambushed me."

Jimmy popped, "We weren't part of ambushing you! Like I was telling you, we..."

Rebekah held up one hand and Jimmy heeded, planting his fists on his hips.

She beckoned to Trey. "Why don't you come upstairs and see for yourself? Mosby has been asking after you."

Trey hesitated then took a step toward the porch. Jimmy flanked him like a prison guard. Trey tossed the reins of his horse at Jimmy, who caught them instinctively. Another look from Rebekah stayed Jimmy, although his eyes protested, telling her he wanted to make sure Trey Wallace didn't try anything.

Doctor McKinnon met her eyes with the same concern. She shook her head, indicating she would handle this alone.

Rebekah escorted Trey up the stairs and down the hall to Mosby's room where the door stood open. She motioned Trey inside as she spoke to Mosby.

"Here's that ruckus we heard."

Trey stepped across the threshold, his hands in his back pockets as he glanced at Rebekah then Mosby. He looked uncomfortable at the cordial treatment, and with facing the wounded man stretched out on the bed.

Mosby nodded at him. "Ain't had a chance to thank you proper for saving my life."

Rebekah moved out and down the hall, giving the men privacy. It was hard enough for them to talk about their feelings. They didn't need a witness.

A few minutes later, Trey came out of the room, head down like he'd been given a lot to think about.

He took a few steps and then his head came up, realizing Rebekah was in the hallway waiting for him. Distain flashed in his eyes before they softened into the boyish look she'd known when treating him years ago. He licked his lips, his jaw not letting him have free movement.

"I appreciate you letting me see him. Guess he'll pull through all right?"

Rebekah nodded. "Thanks to you. But Trey, may I ask for your help? I need it. Really."

Trey's eyebrows furrowed, and he gave her a look, asking what in the world a refined, established woman doctor could possibly need from him.

Rebekah started slowly walking toward the stairs. Trey came alongside her. "You see, for many years, I worked to become a doctor for my people on the Omaha Reservation. I was practicing there along with a colleague. The reservation spans many miles and thousands of people that we were treating. But something happened one night that destroyed everything I had worked for. As a result, I was driven from the reservation with the threat that if I ever returned to practice medicine, I would be forever barred from there."

Rebekah halted and closed her eyes. She'd spoken of this out loud to so few people. Maybe that was why the pain burned intensely in her heart now.

She opened her eyes to find Trey watching her, confusion and a hint of compassion in his expression. She had made the right decision to share this with him.

"I've always known if I returned, even to visit my family, there would be a need, some crisis I would be obliged to treat, and therefore face the consequences. I have not been back, and have lived with a shattered heart even as I sought out anyone I could possibly help with my healing skills."

Rebekah faced him square on, putting her own pain aside for a moment to observe his jaw. She reached out and pressed against his joints with her fingertips. He flinched and started to move away. Rebekah released the pressure, letting him make the choice.

He stilled and Rebekah pressed again. She examined his jawline with her fingers, spending several minutes working it and his lower jaw, massaging it. The joint finally popped, and Trey winced, pulling away, eyes closed. Then he opened them and worked his jaw.

He stared at her, shocked. "You fixed it."

Rebekah smiled. It never ceased to amaze her how surprised people were that this Indian woman doctor actually knew what she was doing.

Trey's eyes melted from surprise...to shame...to respect.

"I always liked you, Doc Beck. You saved my life once and I never really thanked you for it. I don't know what you getting banned from the reservation has to do with me, but I'll help anyway I can."

Rebekah swallowed. "If you really and truly mean that...I need you to help me find out what happened with Lilly Butler at her school."

There was nothing quite like riding across the Great Plains in summertime. It was a rugged country filled with all of God's natural beauty, strokes of a true Artist in every layer from the cerulean blue sky to the softened green grasslands.

But this day, beyond the Medicine Bow Mountains, a dark indigo thunderhead was building steam and casting a shadowy pallor over the golden meadows. It was toward that thundercloud that Rebekah and Trey rode.

Jimmy and Doctor McKinnon objected to her riding off alone with Trey, especially with the coming storm seen from miles and miles away. Rebekah assured them she knew what she was doing.

She did.

What Trey told her in their conversation would change Lilly Butler's life. And Rebekah's in the process.

They rode side-by-side at a steady lope, mindful of prairie dog holes. When they gained the foothills, Rebekah slowed her horse and allowed Trey to take the lead on the slim trail. They navigated foothills, then followed a ledge around the base of the mountain.

The trail was precarious, showing signs of rockslides, but also evidence of a well-used path.

Trey had told Rebekah how he and Lilly would come there when they were friends as youths, until Dean Wallace found out. He shocked Trey by telling him that Glenn Butler had caused his mother's death, and warned him to stay away from that family forever. Trey hadn't spoken a civil word to Lilly Butler since.

But it was his own confession that had Rebekah risking her neck to ride this trail on the chance that Lilly Butler might have taken it that day. Trey said he spotted her on his way to the McKinnon Ranch, though they had given one another a wide berth.

The trail disappeared between two boulders the size of a small cabin on each side. Rebekah let her horse pick his way carefully through the passage. When it opened up, she caught her breath. There was the island Trey told her about.

But he hadn't told her how beautiful it was.

In this cup-like ravine, the pines were a deep green against a steep hill covered with yellow flowers and sunshine. The river rolled at a hearty clip down the mountain, encasing the scrap of land. The clear water showed multi-colored river rocks beneath gentle whitecaps.

It was another world, a place of escape and rest. A haven from troubles.

Lilly Butler's saddled horse was tied to brush at the edge of the tree line. The young woman sat atop a cluster of boulders on the island overlooking the river, her back partly to them. She hadn't seen the intruders yet.

Trey led the way through the shallow of the river, his horse high stepping through the chilled mountain water. Rebekah followed and they splashed onto the rock beach of the island.

Lilly's horse whinnied and their horses responded, catching the young woman's attention. Her hand went to the rifle that lay on the rock beside her. When she saw it was Trey Wallace and Doctor Rebekah LaRoche, her hand tightened around the stock.

Rebekah dismounted next to the girl's horse and let Trey tie them both. She lifted her skirts to navigate over the rocky terrain and up the dry dirt path to where Lilly now stood. She'd left the rifle laying on the rocks.

Rebekah waited until Trey joined them before speaking. "Lilly, I've come to talk to you about something that involves both our futures."

Lilly sucked in a breath, looking between Trey and Rebekah. "I'm not supposed to speak to either of you. And I don't want to, either."

Her voice held the confident, authoritative ring to it that had convinced Rebekah to write the recommendation letter for her admission into law school. The young woman could hold her own in a court of law, even if she was the only woman present.

Lilly squatted and picked up the rifle, her hand tight over the stock and finger hovering near the trigger. She started for the trail leading off the boulders, but Trey stepped in front of her.

"Lilly Butler, you are going to stand here and listen to what Doc Beck has to say, and what I have to say, too. I got y'all both in trouble and I'm here to get you out."

Lilly stepped back as though he struck her, but she pinched her lips together and said nothing.

This wasn't starting off on the right foot, but Rebekah could expect no better with two feuding families. She spoke to Lilly. "I know you were expelled from law school. Mrs. Haberdasher sent me a letter."

Lilly's face paled and her hand shook. She fumbled her rifle. Trey grabbed it and pulled it from her loose fingers. Lilly didn't try to stop him.

"I didn't do it, Miss Rebekah. I didn't cheat! I never would. I despise those who use the law to their advantage."

The color had come back to her face, fire in her eyes now as she leveled her gaze on Trey. "Like Dean Wallace did. Your father stole everything from mine."

Trey shifted his jaw then adjusted it back. "I know."

He gripped her rifle with both hands, holding it stiffed armed. "My pa hated yours ever since the war. He wanted to take everything, and he did. Taught me to do the same, but he crossed the line too many times, and so did I."

Trey swallowed and looked to Rebekah. He was tough, but there was a plea in that look. He wanted her to tell Lilly Butler what he'd done. But this was his confession to make.

Rebekah nodded encouragement for him to go on. Trey Wallace wasn't a coward. He wouldn't run from this confession.

He faced Lilly. "I knew a girl there at the college, and that y'all stayed at the same boarding house. She needed money to finish school because her family had fallen on hard times and she wrote asking me for help. I told her I would, if she snuck your teachers' papers into your room and sent an anonymous letter so they would find them."

Lilly's eyes opened round, her mouth agape like a fish on the rock bank. Then she snapped her mouth closed and her hand flashed out, striking Trey across his sore jaw.

He winced but held his place. Lilly shrieked, "How dare you! You ruined my life!"

Rebekah put her arm around Lilly's shoulders, holding her close as the young woman shook, tears rolling down her cheeks.

Trey met Lilly's eyes again. "I just wanted you to feel what you and your daddy always accused my pa of—cheating his way through life."

Rebekah squeezed Lilly tighter. "I'm going to write a letter to Mrs. Haberdasher and explain what happened. However many letters it takes and whatever it costs, I'm going to see you reinstated to finish your law degree. I still want you to become the first female lawyer in the state of Wyoming. That is, if you're willing to fight for it."

Lilly straightened, pulling away from Rebekah as she wiped her cheeks with both palms. "I'm willing."

Then her head jerked up and she looked between Rebekah and Trey, eyes wide. "But we have to stop him. Now!"

Rebekah grabbed Lilly's hand, trying to calm her. "Who? Stop who from doing what?"

Lilly gripped Rebekah's hand in both of hers. "My father. He plans to burn the Wallace place down today."

CHAPTER 13

Wind ripped wildly through the narrow valley, creating a funnel that made Rebekah feel as though she were in a deadly hurricane. Saplings bowed to the ground, finding a strange bed among the rocks. Rebekah's bun had torn loose and her hair flew straight behind her as she rode full gallop alongside Trey through the valley floor, taking a shortcut from the island oasis to reach the Wallace home before it was too late.

After Lilly's news, Rebekah sent the young woman to the McKinnon Ranch to tell Doctor McKinnon what was happening, and to fetch Laramie Jones and the crew to stop it if they could.

Thunder rippled around her, shaking Rebekah to the core. She'd never known such rumbling. It wouldn't stop.

She pulled her horse to a trot then a walk. Using one hand, she held her hair away from her eyes to look around the narrow valley. Trey circled his horse, the animal tossing her head. Rebekah could see Trey shouting something at her, but the wind snatched his words away. She twisted in the saddle, thunder still shaking her.

Or was it thunder?

Rebekah jumped off the horse and knelt on the ground. She put her bare palms flat against the prairie grasses, working her fingers into them until she could feel the earth beneath. It vibrated through her fingertips and her entire being.

It wasn't thunder.

Trey spurred his horse back to her and swung off before the animal came to a stop, shouting, "What is it?"

Rebekah leaned back on her heels, using her arms to keep her skirts down in the powerful wind. She shouted to be heard above its roar. "I'm not sure…"

She trailed off at the sight over Trey's shoulder. She gasped.

Trey shifted to look. He froze.

A herd of 300 horses was charging in from the trail ahead and pouring into the valley, churning like a locomotive toward them.

Rebekah grabbed Trey's arm and shook it to snap him into action. He quickly gathered his reins and swung aboard his horse without using the stirrup. Rebekah mounted and they were off before either were seated. They galloped at an angle, heading for the trees to take shelter among the boulders, trying to stay ahead of the herd running mad through the valley.

But the humans wouldn't make it in time.

Rebekah called to Trey, "Stay with me!"

She shifted her direction to head straight up the valley in front of the horse herd. Though he may have thought she was crazy, Trey followed her.

They approached the end of the valley. The riderless horses were catching up. A stand of trees lay ahead.

Rebekah looked over her shoulder and tugged on her horse's reins, slowing his flat out run.

Trey shouted, "Whip him up! They're gaining!"

Yes. They were. Rebekah slowed her horse a touch more as the first wave of the stampede closed in on her.

She faced forward again, loosening the reins and letting her horse pick his path through the copse of trees. His instinct took over and Rebekah gripped the saddle horn with both hands as the rush of horse flesh engulfed her.

CHAPTER 14

The storm proved to be a lot of bragging and swagger. No rain fell, no real damage done even though it seemed like the storm itself carried death.

It was just a bunch of bluster, something Rebekah hoped proved true of the situation she and Trey trotted into at the barnyard of the Wallace ranch.

Lined up in front of the house was Dean Wallace flanked by his men. Opposite him, mounted and rifles out and cocked, was Glenn Butler and his crew. Several of them carried lit torches.

In between the parties, holding the line of fire, was Doctor McKinnon astride his big black mare, Laramie Jones at his side. Jimmy, Steve, and several other hands from the McKinnon Ranch were spread out behind them.

Rebekah slowed her horse, but kept moving at a steady clip until she was in the middle with Doctor McKinnon, glancing to each side of the feuding ranchers.

Trey stayed with her and Rebekah didn't miss the look his father gave him. But Dean Wallace directed his first shot of words at Rebekah. "You get out of here, woman. I told you before, we need a doctor, I'll send for one. You got no business here otherwise."

Rebekah's gaze swept all the faces, wondering about the one missing. She answered Wallace, "Be that as it may, I cannot ride away when I have a key to stopping this bloodshed."

Butler, sitting ramrod straight on his palomino, spat, "You stay out of this, and while we're at it, you leave my daughter alone once and for all."

Rebekah shifted her attention to him, but not before she caught Doctor McKinnon's eye. He gave her a slight nod.

Rebekah said to Butler, "Your daughter is the key. Where is she?"

Butler shouted, "She's got nothing to do—"

"I'm right here!" The tentativeness was gone from Lilly's voice as she appeared out of the Wallace house.

She stood on the porch behind the Wallace crew, facing her shocked father who loosened his grip on his rifle. "Lilly, you get over here..."

The force was gone from his voice, and tears streamed down Lilly's cheeks. But the steadiness was still there when she said, "It's over, Papa. I told Doctor McKinnon how you stole his and Mr. Wallace's herd of horses to distract from the shame of me being expelled from law school."

Shock reverberated through Rebekah. She shook herself and said, "Those herds are secure in Horseshoe Canyon now. I'm sure Mr. Butler will seek to make restitution to Mr. Wallace and Doctor McKinnon for the trouble. I would say it's time to end this feud peacefully, wouldn't you, gentlemen?"

She looked between Dean Wallace and Glenn Butler. Glenn let the rifle sag on the horn of his saddle, staring across the way at Dean Wallace's rifle still pointed his direction.

Wallace snarled. "You think it's that simple, woman? Well, Butler ought to know, you can only tell the story so long, then the story tells itself. I want everyone here to know, Butler fired the first round of this feud when he tried to kill me on the battlefield, even though we wore the same uniform."

Lilly gasped and Rebekah stared at Glenn Butler. The truth showed in how low he hung his head.

"That's right," Wallace spat. "He knew Julie was in love with me, not him, and was only marrying him for the ranch. Well, he missed his shot, but I didn't. I thought he was dead and had no qualms about taking his fiancé and his ranch when I came back to Wyoming. I never regretted it."

Dean Wallace looked at his son, scuffed and dirty from escaping the stampeding horse.

Rebekah could see something break in Dean Wallace's expression. His rifle barrel lowered to where the muzzle aimed at dirt.

"But I reckon as long as I'm telling truth, might as well tell all of it. Trey, Glenn Butler didn't cause your ma's death. She died in childbirth with you."

Trey blinked his eyes rapidly. Rebekah put a hand on his arm as he sat stiff and tearless. For now.

Doctor McKinnon nudged his horse forward until he was close to Rebekah between the two ranchers. "It sounds like forgiveness is in order all around."

Glenn Butler shoved his rifle into his scabbard and rested his hand on the stock as though all the energy and hate of thirty years had left him depleted.

"Too much has happened to sort it all out," he muttered.

His words struck Rebekah in the heart. Hadn't she recently spoken similar words?

Among the McKinnon crew, she caught Jimmy's eye, and his compassionate gaze fortified her.

She shifted in the saddle toward Glenn Butler. "I beg to differ, sir. Forgiveness is simple. It's just not easy."

A flash of consideration lit Glenn Butler's eyes. A crack was made in the fortified wall between two families and ranches.

And one started in Rebekah. It was time to call on God's strength and open herself to healing.

She whispered, "I forgive the Guerras."

A tender release rocked her soul. She was truly free of Sancho Guerra at last.

CHAPTER 15

Sunday morning cinnamon rolls never tasted quite so good. Rebekah made sure she let Freddy know, although she dodged his direct inquiry of whether or not his food was better than Stubby's. She refused to get in the middle of that feud.

The sweetness of the rolls was made sweeter by the presence of those around the breakfast table that morning. Her Uncle Robert McKinnon was stationed in his place at the head of the table, sipping coffee from his saucer. Laramie Jones sat across from her, Jimmy beside her.

She hoped the Wallace and Butler clans were enjoying their own family breakfasts and that this Sunday's church service would have a presence of peace over it. Though Glenn Butler and Dean Wallace weren't friends, they were closer to a handshake than drawing their guns for the first time in 30 years.

Laramie Jones held the plate of cinnamon rolls out to Jimmy. "You'd better have another one, Just Jimmy. We got a lot of work ahead of us."

Jimmy didn't have to be asked twice. He swiped a cinnamon roll, his fourth if Rebekah hadn't miscounted.

"Yes, sir!"

They did have a great deal of work ahead. As a way of apologizing, Glenn Butler had turned the horse contract over to Doctor McKinnon and Dean Wallace, and the Butler ranch hand who shot Ol' Mosby against Butler's orders was arrested. Then Dean Wallace turned his contract over to Doctor McKinnon, saying he didn't have the resources to fill it. He'd only bid for it to try and best Glenn Butler.

But that left the McKinnon crew with a tall order to fill and not a lot of time to do it. Plus, Mosby decided he wanted to live to get old and was stepping down as head wrangler. He would work around the stable and keep the tack in order, but no more bronc busting for him.

Doctor McKinnon and Laramie were discussing the possibility of future contracts when the front door opened, closed, and Steve appeared. He was dressed in his Sunday suit, hat in hand and a bundle of mail in his other.

Doctor McKinnon waved him in. "Have a seat, Steve. There are some rolls left."

Steve took the seat next to Laramie, dropping his grey felt hat next to the bone china plate. "Yes sir, that is, no sir, Stubby threatened to skin any ranch hand alive with a dull knife if they eat his brother's cooking."

Jimmy gulped the rest of his cinnamon roll as they all chuckled. Steve offered the bundle of mail to Doctor McKinnon, his elbow almost catching Laramie in the jaw.

"Sorry about that, Boss."

Laramie wiped icing off his chin with a grunt. "That's not the best way to start off as the new head wrangler of McKinnon Ranch. "

Steve froze, then gazed around at the serious but pleasant faces at the table. He gulped. "You mean it, Boss? I'm taking Ol' Mosby's place?"

Laramie grinned and slapped him on the shoulder. "As long as you bust broncs and not my jaw."

Steve looked around the table again, then his face broke out in a grin.

"Yippee!"

Steve jumped up from the table, rattling dish ware, spilling Laramie's coffee, and tipping Jimmy's glass of milk. Steve didn't notice as he grabbed his hat and ran out the door, letting loose another whoop as he left.

Doctor McKinnon chuckled. "If he's as exuberant about doing the work as he is about getting the promotion, we ought to have the best head wrangler in the state of Wyoming."

Laramie sopped coffee from the table cloth with his napkin. "Yep, I think we've got ourselves a winner, Doc."

Jimmy and Rebekah dabbed the spilled milk between them. She noticed he looked sad, almost disappointed. Surely he wasn't envious of Steve's promotion?

She asked quietly, "Is everything all right, Jimmy?"

His head came up and he glanced at Laramie and Doctor McKinnon, who were sorting the mail. Jimmy nodded toward the envelopes, answering softly, "Steve and the boys must have went into town last night. They drink and gamble and...things, ma'am. Just was hoping they wouldn't, at least not Steve."

Rebekah set aside the soggy napkin and patted Jimmy's hand. He was trying hard to fit in with the crew, while at the same time living his own convictions.

Doctor McKinnon shuffled more envelopes and held up what look like a telegram. "Ah. Speaking of the state of Wyoming..."

He handed Rebekah the telegram and she scanned it.

Received news from Nebraskan governor. Meeting scheduled for two months' time. —Senator Jeffrey Harris

Rebekah sucked in air, almost causing her to choke. She coughed and caught her breath.

"Oh. This is good news."

Maybe God was truly opening the door for her to return home to the Omaha Indian Reservation in Nebraska.

Doctor McKinnon grunted. "This is odd."

Rebekah pulled her attention away from the telegram to see him offering her an envelope, eyebrows raised. She noted how dirty the envelope was, as if someone had dropped it on a dirt floor and stomped it. There was no return address.

She slit it with the letter opener and pulled out what looked like a circus ticket. What disturbed her, though, was the bloody thumbprint in the middle of the ticket.

Jimmy leaned over her arm to see. "It looks like one of those posters in town about a sideshow that's with the Donovan Brothers Circus. They're having an ape man there."

Rebekah held the ticket closer. Jimmy was right. It was a ticket for a sideshow exhibiting a man with no legs. The bloody thumbprint covered the man's face.

"Let me see." Laramie held out his hand and Rebekah gladly surrendered the filthy ticket.

She would never attend such a display. Who on earth would have sent that to her? And why?

Laramie shook his head and handed it off to Doctor McKinnon. Rebekah cleared her throat, trying to lighten the mood.

"Well, Jimmy, maybe I will be that friend that goes to the circus with you, after all. I certainly have no intention of using *that* ticket!"

They laughed lightly, but a sense of darkness had settled over the bright breakfast. Then Jimmy took up another cinnamon roll.

"When Mr. Stubby finds out I was in here eating his brother's cooking, I reckon he'll skin me alive. Might as well go as fat as a Thanksgiving turkey."

They chuckled as one by one, they stood from the table. It was time to get ready for church.

But Rebekah noticed Doctor McKinnon tucking the strange ticket and envelope into his vest pocket. He would try to find out who sent it to her and why.

It was so good to have people looking out for her.

Dearest reader,

Thank you for reading *Ranch Feud (Doc Beck Westerns Book 5)*. I truly hope it entertained and delighted you!

If you fell in love with the main characters, Rebekah, aka "Doc Beck," and Jimmy, you'll be excited to know book 6, *Bronc Buster*, is available! You can order it on any major retail site or through www.SarahElisabethWrites.com.

Meanwhile, I'd be thrilled if you took a moment to write your thoughts in the form of a review for *Ranch Feud* and post it on your favorite retail outlet and Goodreads. You'll help other readers find this series.

To discover more of my books, free short stories, and to generally stay in touch with me, I invite you to join my VIP reader newsletter. You'll receive a free copy of *The Executions*, book one in my historical fiction *Choctaw Tribune* Series. Please join me through: bit.ly/ChoctawTribune.

Speaking of history, the character of Doc Beck was inspired by Dr. Susan La Flesche (Omaha), who is hailed as the first American Indian to earn a medical degree. In continued research, my mother found Dr. Isabel Cobb (Cherokee), the first woman physician in Indian Territory, in very nearly the same years as Dr. La Flesche.

Lastly, if you're not familiar with my heritage books based on my Choctaw history and culture, you can check them out on my website.

Questions? Send them my way: me@sarahelisabethwrites.com

—Sarah Elisabeth Sawyer
Historical Fiction and Western author
Tribal member of the Choctaw Nation of Oklahoma

CANYON WAR (DOC BECK WESTERNS BOOK 1)

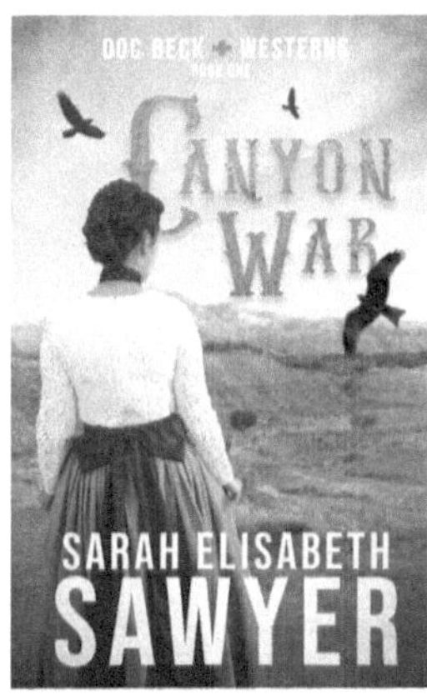

Traveling the West as a female physician, 34-year-old Doctor Rebekah LaRoche is no stranger to trouble. But on her way to New Mexico Territory, an unexpected stay in Amarillo, Texas, leads to confrontation with the Baxter clan – four brothers bred for trouble – and finds Rebekah in deep trouble.

Cattle rancher Clem Baxter's private war over grazing rights in the Palo Duro Canyon turns disastrous, and when the dust settles, one of the Baxter brothers is hurt bad. Clem sends for a doctor, not a woman, but that's what he gets when Rebekah, known as "Doc Beck," arrives at the ranch.

Now held at Clem's ranch against her will, Rebekah must plot to flee through the night with her young friend into the dangers and beauty of the Palo Duro Canyon.

Of Omaha Indian and French descent, Rebekah has always relied on her wits to get her out of any situation. But does that include facing down men willing to die—and kill—for a wild piece of land just as dangerous as any bullet?

***Canyon War* is available on multiple retailer sites.**

♦ ♦ ♦

MISSION BANDITS (DOC BECK WESTERNS BOOK 2)

The Mexican army, a town marshal, and the Sancho Guerra gang are facing off when Doctor Rebekah LaRoche and her new friend, Jimmy, arrive in Zapata, New Mexico Territory. The bandits are holding hostages at Hope Academy, a school for girls located in an old mission outside of town, and Rebekah feels compelled to act—she was sent to the school to modernize the infirmary, not see the innocent occupants murdered.

The notorious and charismatic bandit, Sancho Guerra, led his band of men on a pillaging spree from Mexico to the mission and has proven his indifference to killing, prepared for any tricks the army or the Zapata town marshal throw at him.

But he isn't prepared for Rebekah, and now the Mexican army colonel wants her to do something terrifying—enter the mission and help with the capture of the deadliest men in the territory.

***Mission Bandits* is available on multiple retailer sites.**

♦♦♦

GRAVE ROBBERS (DOC BECK WESTERNS BOOK 3)

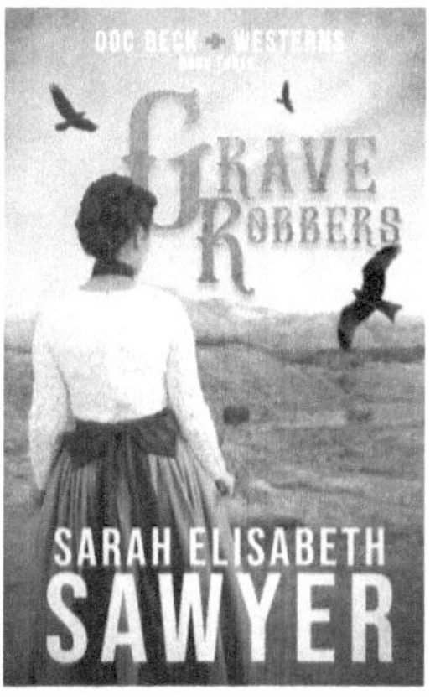

"You swing just as high for killing one as you do three."

Called on to perform an autopsy for a murder case, Doctor Rebekah LaRoche and Just Jimmy find themselves as unlikely detectives in a town with too many secrets.

One of the bandits who held the old mission and Rebekah hostage is accused of murdering Ruby Palmer, a young woman who took some of those secrets with her in death. When Rebekah discovers them during the autopsy, she must fight to prove her former captor is innocent. But she soon learns truth isn't something this town welcomes.

There isn't one straight shooter in the lot—the corrupt sheriff, judge, and leading townsmen are ready to lynch the bandit with hardly a trial. The only man Rebekah partly trusts is Deputy Thad Biggins. But what secret is driving him?

With the whole town against her, Rebekah finds herself at a crossroads: Let the bandit guilty of many crimes hang for one he didn't commit; or prove his innocence by robbing Ruby Palmer's grave.

Grave Robbers is available on multiple retailer sites.

◆ ◆ ◆

DESERT CAPTIVE (DOC BECK WESTERNS BOOK 4)

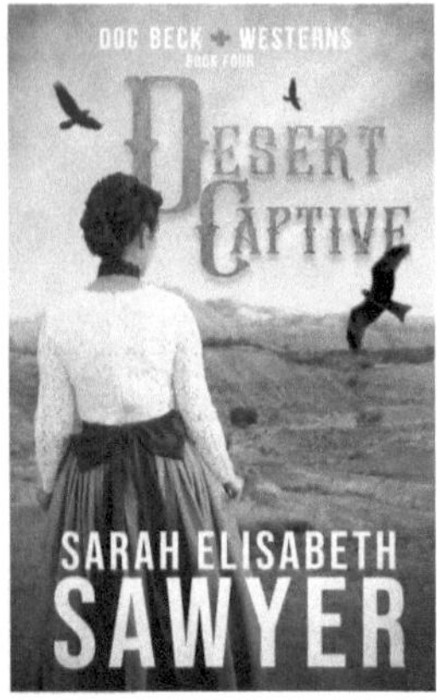

If thou knewest the gift of God...thou wouldest have asked of him, and he would have given thee living water...

There comes a time when one questions every decision they've made in life. That moment is here for Doctor Rebekah LaRoche when she is taken captive by her nemesis, the bandit Sancho Guerra, and spirited across the desert to a hidden village in Mexico.

With no hope of rescue, Rebekah must earn a place among the families of bandits as a medical doctor until she can devise a way to reach the top of the road leading out of the valley—without being shot by the three sets of guards.

Little does Rebekah know that her long-time friend, Laramie Jones, is on his way to attempt a hopeless rescue. If she knew his plans, she'd beg him to stay away: no one has ever penetrated the bandits' valley and lived to tell about it.

With factions closing in all around her, time is ticking down toward an explosive conclusion, and Rebekah will have to draw on her greatest strength yet to survive.

Desert Captive is available on multiple retailer sites.

◆ ◆ ◆

BRONC BUSTER (DOC BECK WESTERNS BOOK 6)

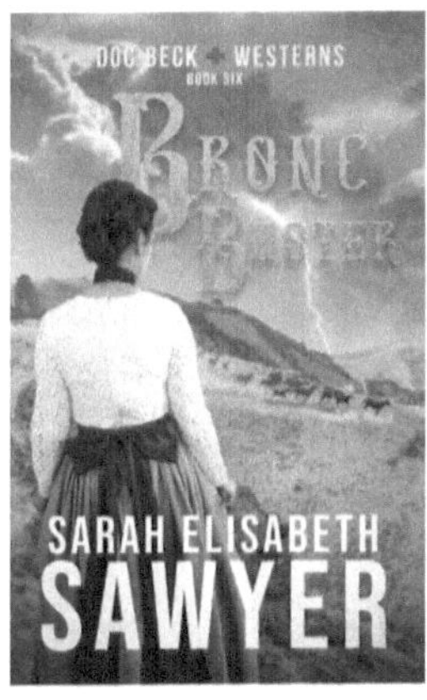

"Sometimes trail dust is thicker than blood."

There's nothing Just Jimmy wants more than to fit in with his new outfit on the McKinnon Ranch, and it's what Doctor Rebekah LaRoche needs, too—another piece in the puzzle of her returning to the Omaha Indian Reservation. But jealousy, a pressing contract with the U.S. Calvary, and soap soup quickly put Jimmy at odds with Steve Bowers, the new head wrangler.

Still shy of the horses they need and facing the looming contract deadline, Steve makes the bold suggestion to catch and break wild mustangs—except Jimmy and Steve aren't the only ones taking care of business in the rugged heart of the Medicine Bow Mountains.

When Jimmy stumbles upon orphaned triplets surviving off the mountain with their flock of sheep and trusty border collie, he must face not only their uncle's drunken rage and false accusation of rustling sheep —but a dark shadow from his own past.

Jimmy has a kind of wound Rebekah can't begin to heal until she understands what shaped the young man who has become her loyal companion. But are either of them prepared for a day when he will no longer be by her side?

Bronc Buster is available on multiple retail sites.

♦♦♦

THE GUNMAN (DOC BECK WESTERNS BOOK 7)

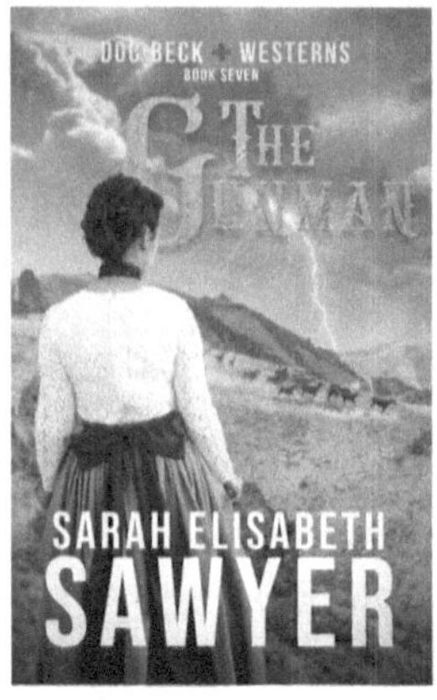

"Whatever you do, stay out of trouble."

The echo of Doctor McKinnon's words follow Doctor Rebekah LaRoche on her latest medical mission. But being tasked with escorting an unknown woman to an insane asylum is difficult enough; add in former gunman Cord Johnson, who claims to be the woman's brother, and Rebekah is set on a dangerous path to discover the truth about the silent woman before it's too late.

Cord Johnson's violent reputation haunts him on his quest to keep a promise made to his sister—a promise he is determined to keep after breaking so many. All he wants to do is to take Ella home to the farm their father left them and live in peace. But when a rogue U.S. marshal arrests him for murder and Doctor Rebekah LaRoche takes off with his sister, Cord must rely on the reputation of his ivory handled six-guns.

With an upcoming political meeting to state her case for returning home to the Omaha Indian Reservation, the last thing Rebekah needs is to get tangled up with a gunman and a lost woman who is unable to speak for herself. But could Cord Johnson be telling the truth? Is Rebekah set to commit the emotionally distraught woman to an asylum that will separate a family forever?

The Gunman is available on multiple retail sites.

◆ ◆ ◆

APE MAN (DOC BECK WESTERNS BOOK 8)

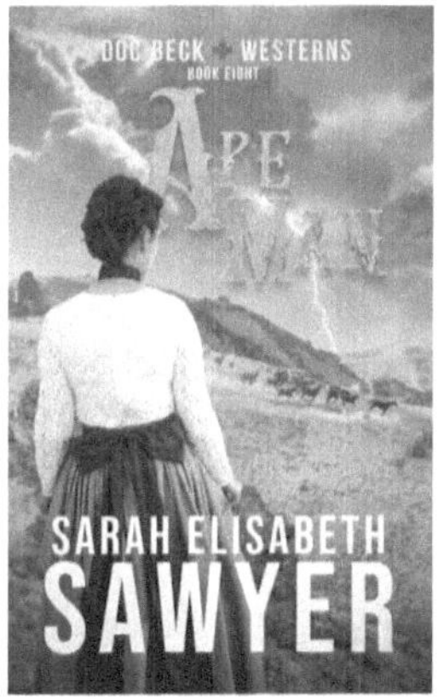

"He's dead."

When Doctor Rebekah LaRoche makes the pronouncement in Senator Jeffrey Harris' office, her world is rocked by the death—and the note found beside the deceased. It's addressed to her personally: an ominous warning that those in her life always end up worse off because of her.

While the Donavan Brothers Circus rolls into Centennial Ridge, Wyoming, a murderous stalker tracks Rebekah's every move and targets those she loves. Death and near-death follow her in a terrifying sequence. But when Just Jimmy finds himself in the stalker's crosshairs, Rebekah unravels, ready to give up her quest to return home to the Omaha Indian Reservation for fear of endangering her relatives there.

Nowhere is truly safe for Rebekah as long as deadly secrets stalk her and tests of faith, regret, and forgiveness culminate in the Medicine Bow Mountains as a single terrifying fight for her own survival. "Doc Beck" has saved many lives—but can she save her own?

Ape Man is available on multiple retail sites.

◆ ◆ ◆

THE EXECUTIONS (CHOCTAW TRIBUNE SERIES, BOOK 1)

Who would show up for their own execution?

It's 1892, Indian Territory. A war is brewing in the Choctaw Nation as two political parties fight out issues of old and new ways. Caught in the middle is eighteen-year-old Ruth Ann, a Choctaw who doesn't want to see her family killed.

In a small but booming pre-statehood town, her mixed blood family owns a controversial newspaper, the *Choctaw Tribune*. Ruth Ann wants to help spread the word about critical issues but there is danger for a female reporter on all fronts—socially, politically, even physically.

But what is truly worth dying for? This quest leads Ruth Ann and her brother Matthew, the stubborn editor of the fledgling *Choctaw Tribune*, to old Choctaw ways at the farm of a condemned murderer. It also brings them to head on clashes with leading townsmen who want their reports silenced no matter what.

More killings are ahead. Who will survive to know the truth? Will truth survive?

The Executions **is available on multiple retailer sites.**

♦ ♦ ♦

TRAITORS (CHOCTAW TRIBUNE SERIES, BOOK 2)

"Someone's going to be king in this territory.

"Nothing to it but a stout heart."

On a mission to bring justice to the outlaw gang that murdered his father and brother, Matthew Teller leaves the *Choctaw Tribune* newspaper for his sister to operate and plunges into an unfamiliar world of darkness and danger. Working inside the coal mines of the Choctaw Nation—one of the most dangerous places in the country—he searches for a man who may have the answers to this six-year-old mystery. But after Matthew uncovers an earth-shattering truth that rocks him to his core, he must decide what right is, and what price he is willing to pay for it.

Ruth Ann Teller knows she can handle publishing the *Choctaw Tribune*—until she loses their biggest advertiser. Now, with Matthew miles away and the future of the newspaper resting squarely on her shoulders, Ruth Ann must make a bold move to keep the newspaper afloat in her brother's absence. She sets it on a course for new success or total disaster.

Striking coal miners. Outlaw gangs. An unsolved crime. And a Choctaw family that fights for one another, and for truth.

◆◆◆

ANUMPA WARRIOR: CHOCTAW CODE TALKERS OF WORLD WAR I

The day I betrayed Isaac, I vowed never again to speak my native language in front of white men.

When America enters the Great War in 1917, Bertram Robert Dunn and his Choctaw buddies from Armstrong Academy join the army to protect their homes, their families, and their country. Hoping to find redemption for a horrible lie that betrayed his best friend, B.B. heads into the trenches of France—but what he discovers is a duty only his native tongue can fulfill.

War correspondent Matthew Teller is ready to quit until an encounter with a fellow Choctaw sets him on a path to write the untold story of

American Indian doughboys. But entrenched stereotypes and prejudices tear at his burning desire to spread truth.

With the Allies building toward the greatest offensive drive of the war, the American Expeditionary Forces face a superior enemy who intercepts their messages and knows their every move. Can the solution come from a people their own government stripped of culture and language?

Anumpa Warrior **is available on multiple retailer sites.**

TOUCH MY TEARS: TALES FROM THE TRAIL OF TEARS

For this collection of short stories, Choctaw authors from five U.S. states came together to present a part of their ancestors' journey, a way to honor those who walked the trail for their future. These stories not only capture a history and a culture, but the spirit, faith, and resilience of the Choctaw people.

Tears of sadness. Tears of joy. Touch and experience them.

Touch My Tears is available on multiple retailer sites.

♦♦♦

TUSHPA'S STORY (Touch My Tears Collection)

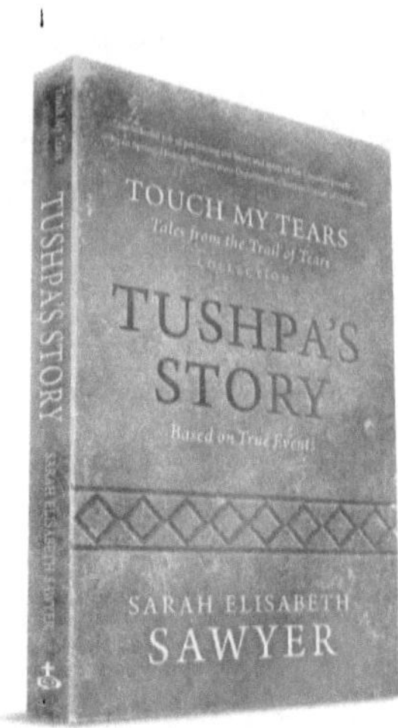

"Protect the book as you do our seed corn. We must have both to survive."

The Treaty of Dancing Rabbit Creek changed everything. The Choctaw Nation could no longer remain in their ancient homelands.

Young Tushpa, his family, and their small band embark on a trail of life and death. More death than life lay ahead.

On their journey to a new homeland, the faith of his father and one book guide Tushpa as he learns what it means to become a man and a leader.

But before long, betrayal from within and without rip at the unity of the band. Can Tushpa help keep his tattered people together? Or will they all be lost to sickness of the mind, body, and spirit on the four hundred mile walk?

A continuation of the anthology *Touch My Tears: Tales from the Trail of Tears*, this story follows an original manuscript written by Tushpa's son, James Culberson.

Tushpa's Story is available on multiple retailer sites.

ABOUT THE AUTHOR

SARAH ELISABETH SAWYER is a story archaeologist. She digs up shards of past lives, hopes, and truths, and pieces them together for readers today. The Smithsonian's National Museum of the American Indian honored her as a literary artist through their Artist Leadership Program for her work in preserving Choctaw Trail of Tears stories. A tribal member of the Choctaw Nation of Oklahoma, she writes historical fiction from her hometown in Texas, partnering with her mother, Lynda Kay Sawyer, in continued research for future works. Learn more at SarahElisabethWrites.com, Facebook.com/SarahElisabethSawyer